It Started at a Wedding...

—

Kate Hardy

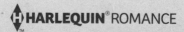

Recycling programs
for this product may
not exist in your area.

ISBN-13: 978-0-373-74335-3

It Started at a Wedding…

First North American Publication 2015

Copyright © 2015 by Pamela Brooks

This edition published by arrangement with Harlequin Books S.A.

For questions and comments about the quality of this book,
please contact us at CustomerService@Harlequin.com.

® and TM are trademarks of Harlequin Enterprises Limited or its
corporate affiliates. Trademarks indicated with ® are registered in the
United States Patent and Trademark Office, the Canadian Intellectual
Property Office and in other countries.

Printed in U.S.A.

Award-winning author **Kate Hardy** lives in Norwich, England, with her husband, two children, one spaniel and too many books to count! She's a fan of the theater, ballroom dancing, posh chocolate and anything Italian. She's a history and science geek, plays the guitar and piano, and makes great cookies (which is why she also has to go to the gym five days a week...).

Books by Kate Hardy

HARLEQUIN ROMANCE

Once a Playboy...
Ballroom to Bride and Groom
Bound by a Baby
Behind the Film Star's Smile
Crown Prince, Pregnant Bride
A New Year Marriage Proposal

Visit the Author Profile page
at Harlequin.com for more titles

To the Harlequin Romance authors,
with much love and thanks for being
such brilliant colleagues and friends—
and for letting me bounce mad ideas off you!

CHAPTER ONE

No.

This couldn't be happening.

The box had to be there.

It *had* to be.

But the luggage carousel was empty. It had even stopped going round, now the last case had been taken off it. And Claire was the only one standing there, waiting with a small suitcase and a dress box—and a heart full of panic.

Where was her best friend's wedding dress?

'Get a grip, Claire Stewart. Standing gawping at the carousel isn't going to make the dress magically appear. Go and talk to someone,' she told herself sharply. She gathered up her case and the box containing the bridesmaid's dress, and went in search of someone who might be able to find out where the wedding dress was. Maybe the box had accidentally been put in the wrong flight's luggage and it was sitting somewhere else, waiting to be claimed.

Half an hour of muddling through in a mixture of English and holidaymakers' Italian got her the bad news. Somewhere between London and Naples, the dress had vanished.

The dress Claire had spent hours working on, hand-stitching the tiny pearls on the bodice and the edge of the veil.

The dress Claire's best friend was supposed to be wearing at her wedding in Capri in two days' time.

Maybe this was a nightmare and she'd wake up from it in a second. Surreptitiously, Claire pinched herself. It hurt. Not good, because that meant this was really happening. She was in Naples with her luggage, her own bridesmaid's dress...and no wedding dress.

There was nothing else for it. She grabbed her mobile phone, found a quiet corner in the airport and called Ashleigh.

Whose phone was switched through to voicemail.

This definitely wasn't the kind of news Claire could leave on voicemail; that would be totally unfair. She tried calling Luke, Ashleigh's fiancé, but his phone was also switched through to voicemail. She glanced at her watch. It was still so early that they were probably in the middle of breakfast and they'd probably left their phones in their room. OK. Who else could she call? She didn't have a number for Tom, Luke's best man. Sammy, her other best friend, who was photographing the wedding, wasn't flying to Italy until tomorrow, after she'd finished a photo-shoot in New York. The rest of the wedding guests were due to arrive on the morning of the wedding.

Which left Ashleigh's brother. The man who was going to give Ashleigh away. The man who played everything strictly by the rules—and Claire had just broken them. Big time. He was the last person she could call.

But he wasn't in Capri yet, either. Which meant she had time to fix this.

What she needed was a plan.

Scratch that. What she *really* needed was coffee. She'd spent the last two weeks working all hours on Ashleigh's dress as well as the work she was doing for a big wedding show, and she'd skimped on sleep to get everything done in time. That, plus the ridiculously early flight she'd taken out here this morning, meant that she was fuzzy and unfocused.

Coffee.

Even thought she normally drank lattes, this called for desperate measures. She needed something strong and something fast. One espresso with three sugars later, Claire's head was clear enough to work out her options. It meant more travelling—a lot more travelling—but that didn't matter. Claire would've walked over hot coals for Ashleigh. She was more than Claire's best friend; she was the sister Claire would've chosen.

She tried calling Ashleigh again. This time, to Claire's relief, her best friend answered her mobile phone.

'Claire, hi! Are you in Naples already?'

'Um, yes. But, Ash, there's a bit of a problem.'

'What's wrong?'

'Honey, I don't know how to soften this.' There wasn't a way to soften news like this. 'Is Luke with you?'

'Ye-es.' Ashleigh sounded as if she was frowning with concern. 'Why?'

'I think you're going to need him,' Claire said.

'Now you're really worrying me. Claire? What's happened? Are you all right?'

'I'm fine.' Claire had no option but to tell her best friend the news straight. 'But I'm so sorry, Ash. I've really let you down. Your dress. It's gone missing somewhere between here and London.'

'What?'

'I've been talking to the airline staff. They phoned London for me. They said it's not in London, and it's definitely not in Naples. They're going to try and track it down, but they wanted us to be prepared for the fact that they might not be able to find it before the wedding.'

'Oh, my God.' Ashleigh gave a sharp intake of breath.

'I know. Look—we have options. I don't have time to make you another dress like that one, even if I could get the material and borrow a sewing machine. But we can go looking in Naples and find something off the peg, something I can maybe tweak for you. Or I can leave the bridesmaid's dress and my case here in the left luggage, and get the next flight back to London. I'm pretty much the same size as you, so I'll Skype you while I try on every single dress in my shop and you can pick the ones you like best. Then I'll get the next flight back here, and you can try the dresses on and I'll do any alterations so your final choice is perfect.'

Except it wouldn't be perfect, would it?

It wouldn't be the dress of Ashleigh's dreams. The dress Claire had designed especially for her. The dress that had gone missing.

'And you'll still be the most beautiful bride

in the world, I swear,' Claire finished, desperately hoping that her best friend would see that.

'They lost my dress.' Ashleigh sounded numb. Which wasn't surprising. Planning the wedding had opened up old scars, so Ashleigh had decided to get married abroad—and the dress had been one of the few traditions she'd kept.

And Claire had let her down. 'I'm so, so sorry.'

'Claire, honey, it's not your fault that the airline lost my dress.'

That wasn't how Sean would see it. Claire had clashed with Ashleigh's brother on a number of occasions, and she knew that he didn't like her very much. They saw the world in very different ways, and Sean would see this as yet another example of Claire failing to meet his standards. She'd failed to meet her own, too.

'Look, I was the one bringing the dress to Italy. It was my responsibility, so the fact it's gone wrong is my fault,' Claire pointed out. 'What do you want to do? Meet me here in Naples and we'll go shopping?'

'I'm still trying to get my head round this. My *dress*,' Ashleigh said, sounding totally flustered—which, considering that Ashleigh was the calmest and most together person Claire knew, was both surprising and worrying.

'OK. Forget Naples. Neither of us knows the place well enough to find the right wedding shops anyway, so we'll stick with London. Have a look on my website, email me with a note of your top ten, and we'll talk again when I'm back in the shop. Then I'll bring your final choices on the next flight back.' She bit her lip. 'Though I wouldn't blame you for not trusting me to get it right this time.'

'Claire-bear, it's not your fault. Luke's here now—he's worked out what's going on and he's just said he'd marry me if I was wearing a hessian sack. The dress isn't important. Maybe we can find something in Capri or Sorrento.'

Ashleigh was clearly aiming for light and breezy, but Claire could hear the wobble in her best friend's voice. She knew what the dress meant to Ashleigh: the one big tradition she was sticking to for her wedding day. 'No, Ash. It'll take us for ever to find a wedding shop. And what if you don't like what they have in stock? That's not fair to you. I know I'll have something you like, so I'm going to get the next flight back to London. I'll call you as soon as I get there,' she said.

'Claire, that's so much travelling—I can't make you do that.'

'You're not making me. I'm offering. You're my best friend and I'd go to the end of the earth for you,' Claire said, her voice heartfelt.

'Me, too,' Ashleigh said. 'OK. I'll call the spa and move our bookings.'

So much for the pampering day they'd planned. A day to de-stress the bride-to-be. Claire had messed that up, too, by losing the dress. 'I'm so sorry I let you down,' Claire said. 'I'd better go. I need to get my luggage stored and find a flight.' And she really hoped that there would be a seat available. If there wasn't... Well, she'd get to London somehow. Train, plane, ferry. Whatever it took. She wasn't going to let Ashleigh down again. 'I'll call you when I get back to London.'

'Please don't tell me something's come up and you're not going to make it in time for the wedding.'

'Of course not,' Sean said, hearing the panic in his little sister's voice and wondering what was wrong. Was this just an attack of last-minute nerves? Or was she having serious second thoughts? He liked his future brother-in-law enormously, but if Ashleigh had changed her mind about marrying him, then of course

Sean would back her in calling off the wedding. All he wanted was to see Ashleigh settled and happy. 'I was just calling to see if you needed me to bring any last-minute things over with me.'

'Oh. Yes. Of course.'

But she sounded flustered—very unlike the calm, sensible woman he knew her to be. 'Ashleigh? What's happened?'

'Nothing.'

But her response was a little too hasty for Sean's liking. He deliberately made his voice gentle. 'Sweetie, if there's a problem, you know you can always talk to me. I'll help you fix it.' OK, so Ashleigh was only three years younger than he was, and he knew that she was perfectly capable of sorting out her own problems—but he'd always looked out for his little sister, even before their parents had been killed in the crash that had turned their lives upside down six years ago. 'Tell me.'

'The airline lost my dress,' Ashleigh said. 'But it's OK. Claire's gone back to London to get me another one.'

Sean paused while it sank in.

There was a problem with his sister's wedding.

And Claire Stewart was smack in the middle of the problem.

Why didn't that surprise him?

'Wasn't Claire meant to be bringing the dress with her?' he asked.

'It wasn't her fault, Sean.'

No. Of course not. It would never be Miss Follow-Your-Heart's fault that something went wrong and everyone else had to pick up the pieces.

But he wasn't going to spoil his sister's wedding by picking a fight with her best friend. At least, not in front of Ashleigh. He fully intended to discuss the matter with Claire herself—sooner, rather than later. 'OK. Is there anything else you need?'

'No, it's fine.'

But his little sister didn't sound fine. She sounded shaky. 'Is Luke there with you?' he asked.

'Yes. He said the dress didn't matter and he'd marry me if I was wearing a hessian sack. He says it's our marriage that matters, not the trappings.'

Sean mentally high-fived his brother-in-law-to-be. And thank God Luke was so sensible and reliable. Ashleigh's last boyfriend had been selfish, thoughtless and flaky—and he'd just so happened to be the best friend of Claire's boyfriend at the time. Which figured. Claire always seemed to leave chaos in her wake.

'I could've told you that, sweetheart. Luke's a good bloke and he loves you to bits. Look, I'll be there later tonight, OK? If there's anything you need, anything at all, just call me. And I'm with Luke. Even if you're wearing a hessian sack, you're going to be the most beautiful bride ever.' The bride his father should've been giving away. His throat tightened. If only. But the crash had happened and they'd had to make the best of it ever since. And Sean was determined that his little sister was going to have the wedding she really wanted. He'd *make* it happen.

'Thanks, Sean.' She blew out a breath. 'I'm fine. Really. This is just a little hiccup and Claire's fixing it.'

Yes, Sean thought grimly, because he'd make quite sure that Claire did exactly that.

'See you tonight,' she said.

'See you tonight.'

Sean checked his diary when he'd put down the phone. All his meetings that afternoon could be moved. Anything else, he could deal with in Capri. A quick word with his PA meant that everything would be sorted. And then he called Claire.

Her phone went straight through to voicemail.

So that meant either she was on the phone already, her phone was switched off completely, or she'd seen his name on the screen and wasn't answering because she was trying to avoid him. OK, then; he'd wait for her at the shop. And he'd make absolutely sure that Ashleigh's dress didn't get lost, this time round.

It didn't take Sean long to get to the terraced house in Camden which held Dream of a Dress on the ground floor and Claire's flat on the top storey. Although the sign on the door said 'closed', he could see light inside—meaning that Claire was there, or whoever she'd employed to man the shop in her absence. Either would do.

He rang the doorbell.

No reply.

OK. Play dirty it was, then. This time, he leaned on the doorbell until a figure hurried through to the door.

A figure wearing a wedding dress.

Claire narrowed her eyes at him when she opened the door. Though he noticed that she didn't ask him why he was here. Clearly she had a pretty good idea that he already knew she'd lost his sister's wedding dress and he wasn't happy about the situation.

'I'm Skypeing Ash right now,' she said quietly. 'And I don't want her upset any more today, so can we leave the fight until she's chosen another dress and I've said goodbye to her?'

Claire clearly realised that they were about to have a fight. A huge one. But Sean agreed with her about not rowing in front of his sister. Right now, Ashleigh's feelings had to come first. 'OK.'

'Good. Come in. If you want a drink, feel free to make yourself something. There's tea, coffee and mugs in the cupboard above the kettle, though I'm afraid there's only long-life milk.' She gestured to a doorway which obviously led to the business's kitchen.

'Thank you,' he said. Though he wasn't about to accept any hospitality from Claire Stewart, even if it was do-it-yourself hospitality.

'If you'll excuse me, I have a wedding dress to sort out.' She gave him a level look. 'And I'm modelling the dresses for Ash, which means I'll need to change several times—so I'd appreciate it if you didn't come through to the back until I'm done.'

'Noted,' he said.

She locked the shop door again, still keeping the 'closed' sign in place, and vanished into the back room. Feeling a bit like a spare part—but wanting to know just how Claire had managed to lose a wedding dress—Sean waited in the main area of the shop until she walked back out, this time dressed in faded jeans and a strappy top rather than a wedding dress.

'No coffee?' she asked.

'No.'

She folded her arms. 'OK. Spit it out.'

'Firstly, does Ashleigh actually have a dress?' he asked.

'There are three she likes,' Claire said. 'I'm taking them all over to Capri as soon as I can get a flight. Then she can try them on, and I'll make any necessary alterations in time for the wedding.'

'What I don't understand is how you managed to lose her dress in the first place.' He shook his head in exasperation. 'Why wasn't it with you in the plane?'

'Believe it or not,' she said dryly, 'that was my original plan. I cleared it with the airline that I could put the boxes with her dress and mine in the overhead storage compartments, and if there was room they'd hang Ash's dress on a rail in the stewardesses' cabin. I packed both the dresses in boxes that specifically met the airline's size guidelines. Your waistcoat and cravat, plus Luke's and Tom's, are packed in with my dress.'

So far, so sensible. But this was Claire—the woman who was chaos in high heels with a snippy attitude. 'But?'

'It turned out there were three other brides on the flight. One of whom was a total Bridezilla and demanded that her dress should be the one in with the stewardesses. There was a massive row. In the end, the captain intervened and ordered that all the bridal dresses should go in the hold with the rest of the luggage—even those belonging to people who weren't involved in the argument with Bridezilla. He wouldn't even let us put the dresses in the overhead lockers. The atmosphere on the plane was pretty bad.' She shrugged. 'The airline staff have looked in London and in Naples, and there's no sign of the box with Ash's dress. They're still checking. It might turn up in time. But it probably won't, so these dresses are my contingency plan—because I don't intend to let Ash down. Ever.'

It hadn't been *entirely* Claire's fault, Sean acknowledged. But, at the same time, she *had* been the one responsible for the dress, and right now the dress was missing. 'Why didn't you buy a seat for the dress?'

'They said I couldn't—that if I wanted the dress to come with me, it would have to be treated as additional cabin luggage. Which,' she pointed out, 'is what I organised and what I paid for.' Her blue eyes were icy as she added, 'And, just in case you think I'm perfectly OK about the situation, understand that I've spent weeks working on that dress and I'm gutted that my best friend doesn't get to wear the dress of her dreams—the dress I designed especially for her. But moaning on about the situation isn't going to get the dress back. I'd rather do something practical to make sure Ash's wedding goes as smoothly as possible. So, if you'll excuse me, I have three wedding dresses to pack and a flight to book.' She shrugged again. 'But, if it makes you feel better, do feel free to storm and shout at me.'

Funny how she was the one in the wrong, but she'd managed to make him feel as if *he* were the one in the wrong, Sean thought.

Though she had a point. Complaining about the situation or losing his temper with her wouldn't make the dress magically reappear. And Claire had spent most of today travelling—two and a half hours each way on a plane, plus an hour each way on a train and waiting round in between. Now she was just about to fly back to Italy: yet more travelling. All for his sister's sake.

Claire Stewart was trying—in both senses of the phrase. But maybe he needed to try a bit harder, too.

'Do you want me to find you a flight while you pack the dresses?' he asked.

She looked at him as if he'd just grown two heads.

'What?' he asked.

'Are you actually being *helpful*?' she asked. 'To *me*?'

He narrowed his eyes at her. 'Don't make it sound as if I'm always the one in the wrong.'

'No. That would be me,' she said. 'In your regimented world view.'

'I'm not regimented,' he said, stung. 'I'm organised and efficient. There's a difference.'

Her expression suggested otherwise.

'I was,' he pointed out, 'trying to call a truce and work with you. For Ashleigh's sake.'

She looked at him for a long, long time. And then she nodded. 'Truce. I can do that. Then thank you—it would save me a bit of time if you could find me a flight. I don't care which London airport it's from or how much it costs—just let me know as soon as they need paying and I'll come to the phone and give them my credit card details. But please put whichever airline in the picture about what happened to the dress this morning, and I want cast-iron guarantees that *these* dresses are going to make it out to Italy with me. Otherwise I'll be carving their entire check-in staff into little pieces with a rusty spoon.'

He couldn't help smiling. 'Spoons are blunt.'

'That,' she said, 'is entirely the point. Ditto the rusty.'

'You really care about Ashleigh, don't you?' he said.

'Sean, how can you not already know that?' Claire frowned. 'She's been my best friend for more than half my lifetime, since I moved to the same school as her when I was thirteen. I think of Ash practically as my sister.'

Which would technically make her his sister, too. Except Sean didn't have any sibling-like feelings towards Claire. What he felt for Claire was…

Well, it was a lot easier to think of it as dislike. When they weren't being scrupulously polite to each other, they clashed. They had totally opposite world views. They were totally incompatible. He wasn't going to let himself think about the fact that her hair was the colour of a cornfield bathed in sunshine, and her eyes were the deep blue of a late summer evening. And he certainly wasn't going to let himself think about the last time he'd kissed her.

'Of course. I'll get you a flight sorted.'

Though he noticed her movements while he was on the phone. Deft and very sure as she packed each dress in tissue paper to avoid creases, put it inside a plastic cover to protect it from any damage and then in a box. As if she'd done this many times before. Which, he realised, she probably had.

He'd never seen Claire at work before. Apart from when she'd measured the three men in the wedding party for their waistcoats, and that had been at Ashleigh and Luke's house. He'd been too busy concentrating on being polite and anodyne to her for his sister's sake to take much notice of what she was actually doing.

And, OK, it was easy to think of dress designers as a bit kooky and not living in the same world as the rest of the population. The outlandish outfits on the catwalks in Milan and the big fashion shows left him cold and wondering what on earth was going on in the heads of the designers—real people just didn't wear stuff like that. But the woman in front of him seemed businesslike. Organised. Efficient.

Like someone who belonged in his world.

He shook himself. That was just an illusion. Temporary. Claire didn't belong in his world and he didn't belong in hers. They'd be civil to each other over the next few days, purely for Ashleigh's sake, and then they'd go back to avoiding each other.

Safely.

CHAPTER TWO

As CLAIRE WORKED on packing up the dresses, she found herself growing more and more aware of Sean. He looked every inch the meticulous businessman in a made-to-measure suit, handmade shirt, and perfectly polished shoes; as part of her job, Claire noticed details like that. Sean wouldn't have looked out of place on a catwalk or in a glossy magazine ad.

And he was actually helping her—working with her as a team. Which was rarer than a blue moon. They didn't get on.

Apart from a few occasions, and some of those were memories that still had the ability to make Claire squirm. Such as Ashleigh's eighteenth birthday party. Claire's life had imploded only a couple of weeks before and, although she'd tried so hard to smile and be happy for her best friend's sake, she'd ended up helping herself to too much champagne that evening to blot out the misery that had threatened to overwhelm her.

Sean had come to her rescue—and Claire had been young enough and drunk enough to throw herself at him. Sean had been a perfect gentleman and turned her down, and her adult self was glad that he'd been so decent, but as a teenager she'd been hideously embarrassed by the whole episode and she'd avoided him like the plague for months and months afterwards.

Then there was his parents' funeral, three years later. Claire had been there to support Ashleigh—just as Ashleigh had supported Claire at her own mother's funeral—and she'd glanced across at Sean at a moment when he'd looked utterly lost. Wanting to help, Claire had pushed past the old embarrassment and gone to offer him her condolences. Sean hadn't been quite approachable enough for her to give him a hug, so she'd simply squeezed his hand and said she was sorry for his loss. At the time, her skin had tingled at the contact with his—but the timing was so inappropriate that she hadn't acted on it.

They'd fought again when Ashleigh had decided not to join the family business. Sean had blamed Claire for talking Ashleigh out of what he clearly saw as her duty. OK, so Claire had been a sounding board and helped

Ashleigh work out what she really wanted to do, encouraging her to follow her dreams; but surely Sean had wanted his sister to be happy instead of feeling trapped and miserable in a job she really didn't want to do? And surely, given that his parents had died so young, he understood how short life was and how you needed to make the most of every moment? It wasn't as if being a maths teacher was some insecure, fly-by-night job. And Ash was a really gifted teacher. She loved what she did and her pupils adored her. It had been the right decision.

The problem was, Sean had always been so overprotective. Claire could understand why; he was Ashleigh's elder brother and had been the head of the family since he was twenty-four. But at the same time he really needed to understand that his sister was perfectly capable of standing on her own two feet and making her own way in the world.

She forced herself to concentrate on packing the dresses properly, but she couldn't help noticing the deep tone of Sean's voice, his confidence and sureness as he talked to the airline.

Most of the time Claire didn't admit it, even to herself, but she'd had a secret crush on Sean when she'd been fourteen. Which was half the reason why she'd thrown herself at him at Ashleigh's birthday party, three years later.

Another memory seeped back in. Ashleigh's engagement party to Luke. Sean had asked her to dance; Claire had been well aware that he was only being polite for his sister's sake. Which was the same reason why she'd agreed to dance with him. Though, somewhere between the start and the middle of the song, something had changed. Claire couldn't even blame it on the champagne, because she hadn't been drinking. But something had made her pull back slightly and look up at Sean. Something had made her lips part slightly. And then he'd dipped his head and kissed her.

The kiss had shaken her right to the core. Nobody had ever made her feel like that with a single kiss—as if her knees had turned to mush and she needed to cling to him to keep herself upright. It had panicked her into backing away and cracking some inane joke, and the moment was lost.

Since then, she'd been scrupulously polite and distant with Scan. But in unguarded moments she wondered. Had he felt that same pull of attraction? And what if…?

She shook herself. Of course not. Apart from the fact that her judgement when it came to men was totally rubbish, she knew that

Sean just saw her as his baby sister's super-annoying best friend, the woman he ended up bickering with every time they spoke to each other for more than five minutes. It rankled slightly that he still didn't take her seriously—surely the fact that she'd had her own business for the last three years and kept it going through the recession counted for *something*?

Then again, she didn't need to prove anything to him. She was perfectly comfortable with who she was and what she'd achieved.

She finished packing the last box.

'Any luck with my flight?' she asked when Sean ended his call.

'There's good news and bad,' he said.

'OK. Hit me with the bad first.'

He frowned. 'Why?'

'Because then I've faced the worst, and there's still something good to look forward to.'

He looked surprised, as if he'd never thought of it in that way before. 'OK. The bad news is, I can't get you a flight where they'll take the dresses on board.'

The worst-case scenario. Well, she'd just have to deal with it. 'Then if planes are out, I'll just have to go by train.' She thought on her feet. 'If I get the Eurostar to Paris, there'll be a connecting train to Milan or Rome, and from there to Naples. Though it means I probably won't get to Capri until tomorrow, now.'

'Hold on. I did say there was good news as well,' he reminded her. 'We can fly to Naples from London.'

She frowned, not understanding. 'But you just said you couldn't get me a seat where they'll take the dresses.'

'Not on a commercial flight, no. But I have a friend with a private plane.'

'You have *what*?'

'A friend with a private plane,' he repeated, 'who's willing to take us this afternoon.'

'Us.' The word hit her like a sledgehammer and she narrowed her eyes at him. 'Are you saying that you don't trust me to take the dresses on my own?'

'You need to go to Naples. I need to go to Naples. So it makes sense,' he said, 'for us to travel together.'

She noticed that he hadn't answered her question. Clearly he didn't trust her. To be fair to him, she had already lost his sister's wedding dress—but it hadn't been entirely her fault. 'But don't you already have a flight booked?'

'I cancelled it,' he said. 'I promised Ashleigh I'd be there tonight or I would've offered you my original booking and flown in later. This seemed like the best solution to the problem.'

'You have a friend with a private plane.' She still couldn't get over that one. 'Sean, normal people don't have friends with private planes.'

'You barely accept that I'm human, let alone normal,' he pointed out.

And they were heading towards yet another fight. She grimaced. 'Sorry. Let's just rewind and try this again. Thank you, Scan, for coming to the rescue and calling in whatever favour you had to call in to get me a flight to Naples. Please tell your friend that if he ever needs a wedding dress or a prom dress made, I'll do it for nothing.'

'I'll tell her,' Sean said dryly.

Her. Girlfriend? Probably not, Claire thought. Ashleigh was always saying that Sean would never settle down and never dated anyone for more than three weeks in a row. So maybe it was someone who'd gone to university with him, or a long-standing business acquaintance. Not that she had any right to ask.

'Thanks,' she said. 'So what time does the flight leave?'

'When we want it to, give or take half an hour,' he said. 'My car's outside. I just need to drop it back home and collect my luggage.'

He looked at her. 'You might as well come with me.'

Gee, what an invitation, Claire thought. But she wasn't going to pick a fight with him now. He'd already gone above and beyond. It was for Ashleigh's sake rather than hers, she knew, but she still appreciated it. 'Ready when you are.'

He drove them back to his house and parked outside. His luggage was in the hallway, so it only took a few seconds for him to collect it; Claire noticed that he didn't invite her in. Fair enough. It was his space. Though she was curious to know whether his living space was as organised and regimented as the rest of him.

They took the tube through to London City airport. Claire used the noise of the train as an excuse not to make conversation, and she knew that he was doing exactly the same. Being with Sean wasn't easy. He was so prickly. He had to have a charming side, or he wouldn't have made such a success of running the family business—clients wouldn't want to deal with him. But the sweetness of the toffee that Farrell's produced definitely didn't rub off on him where Claire was concerned.

The check-in process was much faster than Claire was used to; then again, she didn't know anyone with a private plane. It was more the sort of thing that a rock star would have, not a wedding dress designer. The plane was smaller than she'd expected, but there was plenty of room to stretch out and the seats were way, way more comfortable than she was used to. She always travelled economy. This was another world.

'Welcome aboard,' the pilot said, shaking their hands. 'Our flight today will be about two and a half hours. If you need anything, ask Elise.'

Elise turned out to be their stewardess.

And, most importantly, Elise stored the dress boxes where Claire could see them. This time, she could be totally sure that none of the dresses would be lost.

'Do you mind if I…?' Sean gestured to his briefcase.

Claire would much rather work than make small talk with him, too. 'Sure. Me, too,' she said, and took a sketchpad from her bag. She'd had a new client yesterday who wanted a dress at short notice, plus there was the big wedding show in two months' time—a show where Claire was exhibiting her very first collection, and she was working flat out to get enough dresses ready in time. Six wedding dresses plus the bridesmaids' outfits to go with each, as well as colour co-ordinating the groom's outfit with each set. She could really do with an extra twenty-four hours in a day for the next few weeks—twenty-four hours when she didn't need to sleep. But, as that wasn't physically possible, she'd have to settle for drinking too much coffee and eating too much sugary stuff to get her through the next few weeks.

As he worked, Sean was aware of the quick, light strokes of Claire's pencil against her sketchpad. Clearly she was working on some preliminary designs for someone else's dress. When the sound stopped, he looked over at her.

She'd fallen asleep mid-sketch, her pencil still held loosely in one hand, and there were deep shadows beneath her eyes.

Right at that moment, she looked vulnerable. And Sean was shocked by the sudden surge of protectiveness.

Since when did he feel protective about Claire Stewart?

That wasn't something he wanted to think about too closely. So he concentrated on his work and let her sleep until the plane landed. Then he leaned over and touched her shoulder. 'Claire, wake up.'

She murmured something and actually nestled closer, so her cheek was resting against his hand.

It was his second shock of the afternoon, how her skin felt against his. It made him feel almost as if he'd been galvanised. Very similar to that weird sensation when she'd measured him for the waistcoat—even though her touch had been as professional and emotionless as any tailor's, it had made him feel strange to feel the warmth of her fingers through his shirt.

Oh, help.

Sexual attraction and Claire Stewart were two things that definitely didn't go together, in his book.

OK, so there had been that night, all those years ago—but Claire had been seventeen and his mother had dispatched him to rescue the girl and get her safely to bed back at their house. Of course he'd been tempted when she'd tried to kiss him—he was a man, not an automaton—but he also knew that he was responsible for her, and no way would he ever have taken advantage of her.

And the times since when their eyes had met at one of Ashleigh's parties…

Well, she'd normally had some dreadful boyfriend or other in tow. In Sean's experience, Claire's men were always the type who'd claim that artistic integrity was much more important than actually earning a living. Sean didn't have much time for people who wouldn't shoulder their fair share of responsibility and expected other people to bail them out all the time, but he still wouldn't encourage their girlfriend to cheat on them. He'd never made a move.

Except, he remembered with a twinge of guilt, for the night Ashleigh had got engaged to Luke. He'd asked Claire to dance—solely for his sister's sake. But then Claire had looked up at him, her blue eyes huge and her mouth parted, and he'd reacted purely on instinct.

He'd kissed her.

A kiss that had shaken him to the core. It had shaken him even more when he analysed it. No way could he feel like *that* about Claire Stewart. She was his total opposite. It would never, ever work between them. They'd drive each other crazy.

He'd been too shocked to say a word, at first, but then she'd made some terrible joke or other and he'd somehow managed to get his common sense back. And he'd blanked out the memory.

Except now it was back.

And he had to acknowledge that the possibility of something happening between himself and Claire had always been there. Right now, the possibility hummed just a little harder. Probably because he hadn't dated anyone in the last three months—this was a physical itch, he told himself, and Claire definitely wasn't the right woman to scratch said itch. Their approach to life was way too different for it ever to work between them.

'Claire.' This time, he shook her a little harder, the way he would've liked to shake himself and get his common sense back in place.

She woke with a jolt. She blinked, as if not quite sure where she was, and he saw her expression change the second that she realised what had happened. 'Sorry,' she said. 'I didn't intend to fall asleep. I hope I didn't snore too loudly.'

He could tell that this was her way of trying to make a joke and ease the tension between them. Good idea. He'd follow her lead on that one. 'Not quite pneumatic drill mode,' he said with a smile.

'Good.'

Like him, she thanked the pilot and the stewardess for getting them there safely. And then they were in the bright Italian sunshine, so bright that they both needed to use dark glasses. And Sean was secretly glad of the extra barrier. He didn't want Claire guessing that she'd shaken his composure, even briefly.

And no way was he going to let her struggle with three dress boxes. 'I'll take these for you.'

She rolled her eyes. 'They're not that heavy, Sean. They're just a bit bulky.'

'Even so.'

'I can manage.'

Did she think that he was being sexist? 'I'm taller than you and my arms are longer,' he pointed out. 'So it makes sense for me to carry the boxes.'

'Then I'll carry your suitcase and briefcase.'

He'd almost forgotten just how stubborn she could be. But, at the same time, he had a sneaking admiration for her independence. And he always travelled light in any case, so his luggage wouldn't be too heavy for her.

On the way from the plane to the airport terminal, Claire said to Sean, 'Perhaps you can let me have your friend's name and address, so I can send her some flowers.'

'Already done,' he said.

'From you, yes. I want to send her something from *me*.'

'Sure,' he said easily. 'I'll give you the details when we get to the hotel.'

'Thank you.' She paused. 'And I need to pick

up my case and the bridesmaid's dress. I checked them in to the left luggage, this morning.'

'Wait a second.' He checked his phone. 'Good. Jen—my PA—has booked us a taxi from here to Sorrento and arranged the hydrofoil tickets.'

They went through passport control, then collected Claire's luggage. He waited while she checked with the airline whether Ashleigh's original dress had turned up yet. He knew from her expression that there was still no luck.

The taxi driver loaded their luggage into the car. Claire and Sean were sitting together in the back seat. She was very aware of his nearness, and it made her twitchy. She didn't want to be this aware of Sean. And how did you make small talk with someone who had nothing in common with you?

She looked out of the window. 'Oh, there's Vesuvius.' Looming over the skyline, a brooding hulk of a mountain with a hidden, dangerous core.

'You went there with Ashleigh, didn't you?' he asked.

'And Sammy. Three years ago. It was amazing—like nothing any of us had ever seen before. It was what I imagine a lunar landscape would look like, and we squeaked like schoolkids when we saw steam coming out of the vents.' She smiled at the memory. 'I think that's why Ash chose to get married in Capri, because she fell in love with the island when we came here and had a day trip there.'

They both knew the other reason why Ashleigh hadn't planned to get married in the church where she and Sean had been christened and their parents had got married—because their parents were buried in the churchyard and it had been too much for Ashleigh to bear, the idea of getting married inside the church while her parents were outside.

'It's a nice part of the world,' Sean said.

'Very,' Claire replied. She ran out of small talk at that point and spent the rest of the journey looking out of the window at the coastline, marvelling at the houses perched so precariously on the cliffsides and the incredible blueness of the sea. At the same time, all her senses seemed to be concentrating on Sean. Which was insane.

Finally the taxi dropped them at the marina in Sorrento. Claire waited with their luggage while Sean collected their tickets—and then at last they boarded the hydrofoil and were on their way to Capri.

There were large yachts moored at the marina. As they drew closer she could see the buildings lining the marina, painted in brilliant white or ice cream shades. There were more houses on the terraces banking up behind them, then the white stone peak of the island.

Once they'd docked, they took the funicular railway up to the Piazzetta, then caught a taxi from the square; she noticed that the cars were all open-topped with a stripy awning above them to shade the passengers. So much more exotic than the average convertible.

The taxi took them past more of the brilliant white buildings, in such sharp contrast to the sea and the sky. There were bougainvillea and rhododendrons everywhere, and terracotta pots full of red geraniums. Claire had always loved the richness and depth of the colours on the south European coast.

At last, they reached the hotel.

'Thank you for arranging this,' she said as they collected their keys. 'And you said you'd give me your friend's details?' She grabbed a pen and paper, ready to take them down as Sean gave them to her. 'Thanks. Last thing—milk, white or dark chocolate?'

'I have no idea. You're sending her chocolate?'

'You've already sent flowers.' She smiled. 'I

guess you can't really send anyone confectionery, with your business being in that line.' Ad-
mittedly Farrell's specialised in toffee rather
than chocolates, but it would still be a bit of a
faux pas. 'I'll play it safe and send a mixture.'

'Good plan,' he said. 'See you later.'

He'd made it clear that he didn't plan to
spend much time with her. Which suited Claire
just fine—the less time they were in each other's company, the less likelihood there was of
another fight.

She let the bellboy help her carry her luggage to her room. She'd barely set the dress
boxes on the bed in her room when there was
a knock on the door.

'Come in,' she called with a smile, having
a very good idea who it would be.

Ashleigh walked in—physically so like
Sean, with the same dark eyes and dark hair,
but a million times easier to be with and one of
Claire's favourite people in the whole world.
Claire hugged her fiercely. 'Hey, you beauti-
ful bride-to-be. How are you?'

Ashleigh hugged her back. 'I'm so glad to
see you! I can't believe you've been flying
back and forth between England and Italy all
day. That's insane, Claire, even for you.'

Claire shrugged. 'You're worth it. Anyway,
I'm here now.' She held her friend at arm's

length. 'You look gorgeous. Radiant. Just as you should be.'

'And you look shattered,' Ashleigh said, eyeing her closely. 'You were up before dawn to get your first flight here.'

'I'm fine. I, um, had a bit of a nap on the plane,' Claire admitted.

'Good—and you must be in dire need of something to eat and a cold drink.'

'A cold drink would be nice—but, before we do anything else, I need you to try on these dresses so I can get the alterations started.' Claire hugged her again. 'I'm so sorry that it's all gone so wrong.'

'It wasn't your fault,' Ashleigh said loyally.

That wasn't how Sean saw it, but Claire kept that thought to herself.

Ashley tried on the dresses and looked critically at herself in the mirror. Finally, she made her decision. 'I think this one.'

'Good choice,' Claire said.

Thankfully, the dress didn't need much altering. Claire took the dressmaking kit from her luggage and pinned the dress so it was the perfect fit.

'You're not doing any more work on that tonight,' Ashleigh said firmly. 'It's another day and a half until the wedding, and you've been travelling all day, so right now I want you to chill out and relax.'

'I promise you, I plan to have an early night,' Claire said. 'But I still need to check the waistcoats on the men. And I would kill for a shower.' All the travelling had made her feel tired, as well as sticky; running some cool water over her head might just help to keep her awake a bit longer.

'Sort the men's fitting tomorrow after breakfast,' Ashleigh said. 'Just have your shower, then come and meet us on the terrace when you're done. I'll have a long, cold drink waiting for you. With lots and lots of ice.'

'That sounds like heaven,' Claire said gratefully.

When Ashleigh had gone, Claire hung up all the dresses and waistcoats, and had a shower. Then she joined her best friend, her husband-to-be and their best man on the terrace. To her relief, Sean wasn't there.

'He had some phone calls to make,' Ashleigh explained. 'You know Sean. He always works crazy hours.'

Probably, Claire thought, because he'd been thrown in at the deep end when he'd had to take over the family business at the age of twenty-four after their parents had been killed in a car crash. Working crazy hours had got him through the first year, and it was a habit that had clearly stuck. 'Well—cheers,' she said, and raised her glass as the others echoed her toast.

Somehow Claire managed to avoid Sean for most of the next day; their only contact was just after breakfast, when she did the final fitting of the waistcoats and checked that they went perfectly with the suits and shirts. She was busy for most of the day making the last-minute alterations to Ashleigh's dress, and when she was finished Sean was still busy making phone calls and analysing reports.

Then again, the sheer romance of the island of Capri would be wasted on a man like Sean, Claire thought. He was too focused on his work to notice the gorgeous flowers or the blueness of the sea. So much so that she'd half expected him not to join them for the surprise that she and Luke had organised for Ashleigh that evening; when he joined them in the taxi, she had to hide her amazement.

'So where are we going?' Ashleigh asked.

'You'll see. Patience, Miss Farrell,' Claire said with a grin. Actually, it was something that she was looking forward to and dreading in equal measure, but she knew that it was something her best friend would love, so she'd force herself to get over her fears. It was just a shame that Sammy wasn't there to join them as her flight from New York had been delayed. Which meant that, instead of being able to let Sammy defuse the awkwardness between herself and Sean, Claire was going to have to make small talk with him—because she could hardly talk only to the best man and the groom-to-be and ignore Sean completely.

Finally they arrived at the chairlift.

'Oh, fabulous!' Ashleigh hugged Claire and then her husband-to-be. 'I love this place. I didn't think we'd get time to do this.'

'It was Claire's idea,' Luke said with a smile. 'She said sunset at the top of Monte Solaro would be incredibly romantic.'

'Especially because it's outside the usual tourist hours and we'll have the place all to ourselves. I can't believe you arranged all this.' Ashleigh looked thrilled. 'Thank you so much, both of you.'

Twelve minutes, Claire reminded herself as she was helped onto the chair. It would only take twelve minutes to get from the bottom of the chairlift to the very top of the island. She wasn't going to fall off. It was perfectly safe. She'd done this before. Thousands and thousands of tourists had done this before. The chairs were on a continuous loop, so all she had to do was let them help her jump off at the top. It would be *fine*.

Even so, her palms felt slightly damp and she clung on to the green central pole of her chair for dear life. Thankfully, her bag had a cross-body strap, so she didn't have to worry about holding on to that, too. Her hands ached by the time she reached the top, but she managed to get off the chair without falling flat on her face.

Just as she and Luke had arranged, there was a table at the panoramic viewpoint overlooking the *faraglioni*, the three famous vertical columns of rock rising out of the sea. There was a beautiful arrangement of white flowers in the centre of the table, and white ribbons on the wicker chairs. When they sat down, the waiter brought over a bottle of chilled Prosecco and canapés.

'Cheers. To Ashleigh and Luke—just to say how much we love you,' Claire said, lifting her glass, and the others echoed the toast.

'I really can't believe you did this.' Ashleigh was beaming, and Claire's heart swelled. The night before the wedding, when Ashleigh should've been happily fussed over by her mum…Claire had wanted to take her best friend's mind off what she was missing, and she and Luke had talked over the options. The scary one had definitely been the best decision.

'It wasn't just me. It was Luke as well,' Claire said, wanting to be fair. 'It's just a shame Sammy couldn't make it.'

'She'll be here tomorrow,' Tom said confidently.

'You know, some brides actually get married up here,' Ashleigh said. 'Obviously they're not going to walk for an hour uphill in a wedding dress and high heels, so they ride on the chairlift. I've seen photographs where the bride carried her shoes in one hand and her bouquet in the other.'

'And I suppose Claire showed them to you,' Sean said.

Claire didn't rise to the bait, but she wished she hadn't already done the final fitting of his waistcoat, because otherwise she would've had great pleasure in being totally unprofessional and sticking pins into him.

'No,' Ashleigh said. 'Actually, she talked me out of it.'

'Because the design of your dress means you wouldn't fit in the seat properly and I didn't want your dress all creased in the photographs,' Claire said with a smile.

Ashleigh laughed. 'More like because you wouldn't be able to hang on to your shoes and your flowers and cling on to the central bar for dear life all at the same time.'

Claire laughed back. 'OK, so I'm a wuss about heights—but I would've done it if that's what you'd really wanted, Ash. Because it's your day, and what *you* want is what's important.' Her words were directed at her best friend, but she looked straight into Sean's eyes, making it very clear that she meant every word.

He had the grace to flush.

It looked as if he'd got the message, then. Ashleigh came first and they'd put their differences aside for her sake.

Luke and Tom chatted easily, covering up the fact that Claire and Sean were barely speaking to each other. And gradually Claire relaxed, letting herself enjoy the incredibly romantic setting. They watched as the sun began to set over the sea; mist rose around the distant islands as the sky became striped with yellow and pink and purple, making them seem mysterious and otherworldly.

Claire took a few shots with her camera; she knew they wouldn't be anything near as good as Sammy's photographs, but it would at least be a nice memory. She glanced at Sean; he looked as if he was lost in thought, staring out at the sunset. Before she quite realised what she was doing, she took the snap.

Later that evening, back in her hotel room, she reviewed her photographs. There were some gorgeous shots of the sunset and the sea, of Ashleigh and Luke and Tom. But the picture she couldn't get out of her head was the impulsive one she'd taken of Sean. If they'd never met before, if there were no history of sniping and backbiting between them, she would've said he was the most attractive man she'd ever met and she would've been seriously tempted to get together with him.

But.

She'd known Sean for years, he was far from an easy man, and she really didn't need any complications in her life right now.

'Too much Prosecco addling your brain, Claire Stewart,' she told herself with a wry smile. 'Tomorrow, you're on sparkling water.'

Tomorrow.

Ashleigh's wedding day.

And please, please, let it be perfect.

CHAPTER THREE

'MISS STEWART?' THE woman from the airline introduced herself swiftly on the phone. 'I'm very pleased to say we've found the dress box that went missing.'

It took a moment for it to sink in. They'd actually found Ashleigh's original dress?

'That's fantastic,' Claire said. She glanced at her watch. Ashleigh's wedding wasn't until four o'clock. Which meant she had enough time to get the hydrofoil across to Sorrento and then a taxi to the airport to collect the dress, and she'd be back in time to get the dress ready while Ashleigh was having her hair and make-up done. Thankfully, she'd brought her portable steam presser with her in her luggage, so although the dress would be quite badly creased by now, she'd be able to fix it. 'Thank you very much. I'll be with you as soon as possible.'

'And if you could bring some identification

with you, it would be helpful,' the airline assistant added.

'I'll bring my passport,' Claire said. Even before she'd said goodbye and ended the call, she was unlocking the safe in her wardrobe and taking her passport out.

When she went to tell Ashleigh the good news, Sean was there.

'It'd be quicker to get the dress couriered here,' he said.

'I've already lost the dress once. If you think I'm taking the risk of that happening again...' Claire shook her head. 'No chance.'

It also meant she had a bulletproof excuse to avoid Sean for the next few hours. Though that was slightly beside the point. She kissed Ashleigh's cheek. 'I'll text you when I've picked it up and I'm on my way back. But I'll be back well before it's time to have our hair and make-up done, I promise.'

Ashleigh hugged her back. 'I know. And thanks, Claire.'

'Hey. That's what best friends are for,' she said with a smile.

When Claire collected the dress, the box was in perfect condition, so she didn't have to worry that the contents had been damaged in any way. It didn't matter any more where the dress had been; the important thing was that she had it now, and Ashleigh would wear the dress of her dreams on her wedding day.

'Miss Stewart? Before you go,' the airline assistant said, 'I have a message for you. You have transport back to Capri. Would you mind coming this way?'

'Why?' Claire asked, mystified. She'd planned to get another taxi back to Sorrento, and then the hydrofoil across to Capri.

Before the airline assistant could answer, Claire's phone pinged with a message. 'Sorry, would you mind if I check this?' she asked, just in case it was Ashleigh.

To her surprise, the message was from Sean.

Transport arranged. Don't argue. Ashleigh worrying. Need to save time.

Sean had arranged transport for her? She swallowed hard. She knew Sean had done this for his sister's sake, not for hers, but it was still such a nice thing to do.

And the transport wasn't a taxi back to Sorrento. It was a helicopter. And the pilot told her that the flight from Naples to Capri took less time than the hydrofoil from Sorrento to Capri, so Sean had saved her the time of the taxi journey on top of that.

She texted back swiftly. Thank you. Tell her

the dress is absolutely fine. Let me know how much I owe you for the transport. She knew Sean's opinion of her was already low and she was absolutely not going to let him think she was a freeloader, on top of whatever else he thought about her. She'd always paid her own way.

A text came back from him.

Will tell her. Transport on me.

Oh, no, it wasn't. Dress my responsibility, so *I* will pay. Not negotiable, she typed back pointedly. No way was she going to be in debt to Sean.

She'd half expected a taxi to meet her at the helipad, but Sean was in the reception area, waiting for her. He was wearing formal dark trousers and a white shirt—Claire didn't think he actually owned a pair of jeans—but for once he wasn't wearing a tie. His concession to casual dress, perhaps.

He looked gorgeous.

And he was totally off limits. She really needed to get a grip. Like *now*.

'What are you doing here?' she asked.

'Transport,' he said, gesturing to an open-topped sports car in the car park.

She didn't have much choice other than to

accept. 'Thank you.' She looked at him. 'Is Ash OK?'

'She's fine,' he reassured her.

'Good.'

'And I owe you an apology.'

Claire frowned, surprised. Sean was apologising to her? 'For what?'

'Sniping at you last night—assuming that you'd given Ashleigh that crazy idea of getting married at the top of the mountain and going up by chairlift.'

'Given that I'm scared of heights,' she said dryly, 'I was quite happy to talk her out of that one on the grounds of dress practicalities.'

'But you went up on the chairlift last night.'

She shrugged. 'Luke and I wanted to distract her and we thought that would be a good way.'

'Yeah.'

She looked at him. He masked his feelings quickly, but she'd seen the flash of pain in his eyes. On impulse, she laid her hand on his arm. 'It must be hard for you, too.'

He nodded. 'It should be Dad walking down the aisle with her, not me.' His voice was husky with suppressed emotion. 'But things are as they are.'

'Your parents would be really proud of you,' she said.

'Excuse me?' His voice had turned icy.

She took her hand off his arm. 'OK. It's not my place to say anything and I wasn't trying to patronise you. But I thought a lot of your parents. Your mum in particular was brilliant when my mum died. And they would've been proud of the way you've always been there for Ash, always supported her—well, *almost* always,' she amended. To be fair, he'd been pretty annoyed about Ashleigh's change of planned career. He hadn't supported it at first.

'She's my little sister. What else would I do?'

It was a revelation to Claire. Sean clearly equated duty with love, or mixed them to the point where they couldn't be distinguished. And discussing this was way beyond her pay grade. She changed the subject again. 'So how much do I owe you for the flight?'

'You don't.'

'I've already told you, the dress is my responsibility, so I'll pay the costs. But thank you for organising it, especially as it means Ash isn't worrying any more.'

'We'll discuss it later,' he said. 'Ashleigh comes first.'

'Agreed—but that doesn't mean I'm happy to be in your debt,' she pointed out.

'I did this for Ashleigh, not for you.'

'Well, *duh*.' She caught herself before she said something really inflammatory. 'Sean, I know we don't usually get on too well.' That was the understatement of the year. 'But I think we're going to have to make the effort and play nice while we're on Capri.'

He slanted her a look that said very clearly that he didn't believe she could keep it up.

If she was honest, she wasn't sure she could keep it up, either. Or that Sean could, for that matter. But they were at least going to make the effort. Though they had a cast-iron excuse not to talk to each other for the next few minutes, because he needed to concentrate on driving.

She put the dress box safely in the back of the car, took her sunhat from her bag and jammed it on her head so it wouldn't be blown away, then sat in the front seat next to Sean. She still had her dark glasses on from the helicopter flight, so the glare of the sun didn't bother her.

Sean was a very capable driver, she noticed, even though he was driving on the right-hand side of the road instead of the left as he was used to doing in England. The road was incredibly narrow and winding, with no verges and high stone walls at the edges; it was busy with vans and scooters and minibuses, and every so often he had to pull over into the tiniest of passing places. If Claire had been driving, she would've been panicking that the car would end up being scraped on one of those stone walls; but she knew that she was very safe with Sean. It was an odd feeling, having to rely on someone she normally tried to avoid. And even odder that for once she didn't mind.

'Is there anything you need for the dress?' he asked as they pulled up outside the hotel.

'Only my portable steam presser, which I brought with me on my first trip.'

He looked confused. 'Why do you need a steam presser?'

'This dress has been in a box for three days. Even though I was careful when I packed it, there are still going to be creases in the material, and I don't have time to hang the dress in a steamy bathroom and wait for the creases to fall out naturally. And an ordinary iron isn't good enough to give a professional finish.'

'OK. Let me know if you need anything organised.'

He probably needed some reassurance that it wasn't going to go wrong, she thought. 'You can come and have a sneak peek at the dress, if you want,' she said.

'Isn't that meant to be bad luck?'

'Only if you're the bridegroom. Remember that the dress needs pressing, so you won't be seeing it at its best,' she warned, 'but it will be perfect by the time Ash puts it on.'

Sean looked at Claire. Her sunhat was absolutely horrible, a khaki-coloured cap with a peak to shade her eyes; but he supposed it was more sensible than going out bareheaded in the strong mid-morning sun and risking sunstroke.

He wondered if she'd guessed that he wanted reassurance that nothing else was going to go wrong with the dress—just as she'd clearly noticed that moment when the might-have-beens had shaken his composure. She'd been a bit clumsy about it, but she hadn't pushed him to talk and share his feelings. She'd been kind, he realised now, and that wasn't something he associated with Claire Stewart. It made him feel weird.

But, if she could make the effort, then so could he. 'Thanks. I would appreciate that.'

'Let's go, then,' she said.

He followed her up to her room. Everywhere was neat and tidy. Funny, he'd expected the room to be as messy and chaotic as Claire's life seemed to be—even though her shop had been tidy. But then he supposed the shop would have to be tidy or it would put off potential clients.

She put the dress box on the bed. 'Right—how much do I owe you for that flight?'

'We've already discussed that,' he said, feeling awkward.

'No, we haven't, and I don't want to be beholden to you.'

'Ashleigh is my sister,' he reminded her.

'I know, and she's my best friend—but I still don't want to be beholden to you.'

He frowned. 'Now you're being stubborn.'

'Pots and kettles,' she said softly. 'Tell me how much I owe you.'

Actually, he liked the fact that she was so insistent on paying her fair share. It showed she had integrity. Maybe he'd been wrong to tar her with the same brush as her awful boyfriends. Just because she had a dreadful taste in men, it didn't necessarily mean that she was as selfish as they were—did it? 'OK.' He told her a sum that was roughly half, guessing that she'd have no idea how much helicopter transfers would cost.

'Fine. Obviously I don't have the cash on me right at this very second,' she said, 'but I can either do a bank transfer if you give me your account details, or give you the cash in person when we're back in England.'

'No rush. I'll give you my bank details, but making the transfer when you get back to England will be fine,' he said.

'Good. Thank you.' She opened the box, unpacked the dress, and put it on a hanger.

The organza skirt was creased but Sean could already see how stunning the ivory dress was. It had a strapless sweetheart neckline, the bodice was made of what he suspected might be handmade lace, and it looked as if hundreds of tiny pearls had been sewn into it. It was worthy of something produced by any of the big-name designers.

And Claire had designed this for his little sister. She'd made it all by hand.

Now he understood why she'd called her business that ridiculous name, because she was delivering exactly what her client wanted—a dream of a dress.

Clearly his lack of response rattled her, because she folded her arms. 'If you hate it, fine—but remember that this is what Ash wanted. And I'm giving you fair warning, if you tell Ash you hate it before she puts it on, so she feels like the ugliest bride in the world instead of like a princess, then you're so getting the rusty spoon treatment.'

'I don't hate it, actually. I'm just a bit

stunned, because I wasn't expecting it to be that good,' he admitted.

She dropped into a sarcastic curtsey. 'Why, thank you, kind sir, for the backhanded compliment.'

'I didn't mean it quite like that,' he said. 'I don't know much about dresses, but that looks as if it involved a lot of work.'

'It did. But she's worth every second.'

'Yeah.' For a moment, he almost turned to her and hugged her.

But this was Claire 'Follow Your Heart' Stewart, the mistress of chaos. Their worlds didn't mix. A hug would be a bad, bad idea. 'Thanks for letting me see the dress,' he said. 'I'd better let you get on.'

'Tell Ash her dress is here safely, and I'll come and find her the second it's ready.'

He nodded. 'Will do.'

Once Claire was satisfied with the dress, she took it through to Ashleigh's room. Sammy opened the door. 'Claire-bear! About time, too,' she said with a grin. 'Losing the dress. Tsk. What kind of dressmaker does that?'

'Don't be mean, Sammy,' Ashleigh called. 'I'd cuff her for you, Claire, but I have to sit still and let Aliona take these rollers out of my hair.'

Claire hung up the dress, then enveloped Sammy with a hug. 'Hello to you, too. How was your flight?'

'Disgusting,' Sammy said cheerfully, 'but when I've finished taking photographs tonight then I'm going to drink Prosecco until I don't care any more.'

'Hangover on top of jet lag. Nice,' Claire teased. 'It's so good to see you, Sammy.'

'You, too. And oh, my God. How amazing is that dress? You've really surpassed yourself this time, Claire.'

Claire smiled in acknowledgement. 'I'm just glad we got it back.'

The hotel's hairdresser and make-up artist cooed over the dress, too, and then Claire submitted to being prettied up before putting on her own dress and then helping Ashleigh with hers.

Sammy posed them both for photographs on the balcony. 'Righty. I need to do the boys, now,' she said when she'd finished. 'See you at the town hall.'

'OK?' Claire asked when Sammy had gone.

Ashleigh gulped. 'Yes. Just thinking.'

'I know.' It would be similar for Claire, if she ever got married: she'd be missing her mum, though her dad would be there—*if* he approved of Claire's choice of man—and her mum's family would be there, with Ashleigh and Sammy to support her.

Not that Claire thought she'd ever get married. All the men she'd ever been involved with had turned out to be Mr Wrong. Men she'd thought would share her dreams, but who just couldn't commit. Men who'd been so casual with her emotions that she'd lost trust in her judgement.

'But I think they're here in spirit,' Claire said softly. 'They loved you so much, Ash. And Luke can't wait to make you his bride. You've got a good guy, there.'

'I know. I'm lucky.' Ashleigh swallowed hard.

'Hey. If you cry and your make-up runs, Sean will have my guts for garters,' Claire said. She went into a dramatic pose. 'Help! Help! Save me from your scary big brother!'

To her relief, it worked, and Ashleigh laughed; she was still smiling when Sean knocked on her door to say they needed to go.

CHAPTER FOUR

SEAN HAD ALREADY seen the dress—albeit not at its best—but seeing his little sister wearing it just blew him away. The ivory dress empha-sised Ashleigh's perfect hour-glass shape by skimming in at the waist, then falling to the floor in soft folds. Her dark hair was drawn back from her face and pinned at the back as a base for her veil, and then flowed down in soft curls. She wore a discreet and very pretty tiara with sparkling stones and pearls to re-flect the pearls in the bodice. And finally she was carrying a simple posy of dusky lavender roses, the same colour as Claire's dress; the stems were tightly bound with ivory ribbon.

'You look amazing, Ashleigh,' he said. 'Re-ally amazing.'

Then he glanced at Claire. Again, he was shocked. He hadn't seen the bridesmaid's dress before, though he'd had a fair idea that it would be dusky lavender, the same colour as his waistcoat and the rose in his button-hole. Although it, too, was strapless and had a sweetheart neckline, it was much plainer than Ashleigh's dress and ended at the knee. Claire's hair was dressed in a similar style to his sister's, though without a veil and with a discreet jewelled headband rather than a tiara. Her roses were ivory rather than lavender, as a counterpoint to the bride's bouquet, and her satin high heels were dyed to match her dress.

If he'd seen her across a crowded room as a complete stranger, he would've been drawn to her immediately. Approached her. Asked her out.

He pushed the thought away. This was Claire. He *did* know her. And, if they hadn't made a truce for Ashleigh's sake, they would've been sniping at each other within the next five minutes. She was absolutely not date material.

'Ready?' he asked.

'Ready,' they chorused.

The official civil ceremony was held at the town hall in Anacapri. Only the main people from the wedding party were there: Ashleigh and Luke, with Luke's best friend, Tom, as the best man, Claire as the bridesmaid and one of the witnesses, and himself as the other witness. Sammy was there, too, to take photographs.

After everything had been signed, the two

open-topped cars took them to the private villa where the symbolic ceremony was being held and the rest of their family and friends were waiting to celebrate with them.

Luke and Tom went ahead to wait at the bridal arch, which was covered with gorgeous white flowers.

Then Ashleigh stood at the edge of the red carpet, her arm linked through Sean's. He could feel her trembling slightly. Nervous, excited and a little sad all at the same time, he guessed. 'Ashleigh, you're such a beautiful bride,' he said softly. 'Our parents would be so proud of you right now.'

Ashleigh nodded, clearly too overcome to speak, and squeezed his arm as if to say, 'You, too.'

'Come on. Let's get the party started,' he said, and gave the signal to the traditional Neapolitan guitar and mandolin duo.

Their version of Pachelbel's 'Canon' was perfect. And Sean was smiling as he walked his little sister down the aisle to marry the man she loved.

Claire had seen the photographs and knew that the garden where Ashleigh and Luke were getting married was spectacular, but the photographs really hadn't done the place justice.

The garden was breathtaking, overlooking the sea; lemon trees grew around the edge of the garden, their boughs heavy with fruit, and the deep borders were filled with rhododendrons and bougainvillea. There seemed to be butterflies everywhere. A symbol of good luck and eternal love, she thought.

She took the bouquet from Ashleigh and held it safely during the ceremony, and she had to blink back the tears as Ashleigh and Luke exchanged their vows, this time in front of everyone. She glanced at Sean, who was standing beside her, and was pleased to see that for once he was misty-eyed, too. And so he should be, on Ashleigh's wedding day, she thought, and she looked away before he caught her staring at him.

Everyone cheered when the celebrant said, 'You may now kiss the bride,' and Luke bent Ashleigh back over his arm to give her a show-stopping kiss.

'Let them have it, guys,' Sammy called as Ashleigh and Luke started to walk back down the aisle, and the confetti made from white dried flower petals flew everywhere.

Once the formal photographs had been taken, waiters came round carrying trays filled with glasses of Prosecco. Ashleigh and Luke headed the line-up to welcome their guests; and then, finally, it was time for the meal. Ashleigh had chosen a semi-traditional top table layout, so Claire as the chief bridesmaid was at one end, next to Luke's father. As Sean was standing in for the bride's father, he was at the other end, between Ashleigh and Luke's mother. And there were enough people between them, Claire thought, for them to be able to smile and hide their relief at not having to make small talk.

It was an amazing table, under a pergola draped with white wisteria. Woven in between the flowers were glass baubles, which caught the light from the tea-light candles set in similar glass globes on the table, and reflected again in the mirrored finish of the table. The sun was already beginning to set, and Claire had never seen anything so romantic in her life. And the whole thing was topped off by the traditional Neapolitan guitar and mandolin duo who played and sang softly during the meal.

If she ever got married, Claire thought, this was just the kind of wedding she'd want, full of love and happiness and so much warmth.

Finally, after the excellent coffee and tiny rich Italian desserts, it was time for the speeches. Luke's was sweet and heartfelt,

Tom's made everyone laugh, but Sean's made her blink back the tears.

He really did love Ashleigh. And, for that, Claire could forgive the rest.

The cake—a spectacular four-tier confection, which Claire knew held four different flavours of sponge—was cut, and then it was time for the dancing.

Ashleigh and Luke had chosen a song for their bridal dance that always put a lump in her throat—'Make You Feel My Love'—and she watched them glide across the temporary dance floor. The evening band played it in waltz time, and Claire knew that Luke had been taking private lessons; he was step-perfect as he whirled Ashleigh round in the turns. The perfect couple.

Tradition said that the best man and the chief bridesmaid danced together next, and Claire liked Tom very much indeed; she was pleased to discover that he was an excellent dancer and her toes were perfectly safe with him.

'I love the dresses,' Tom said. 'If I wasn't gay, I'd *so* date you—a woman who can create such utter beauty. You're amazing, Claire.'

She laughed and kissed his cheek. 'Aww, you're such a sweetie, Tom. Thank you. But I wouldn't date you because I have terrible taste in men—and you're far too nice to be one of *my* men.'

He laughed. 'Thank *you*, sweetie. You'll find the right guy some day.'

'If I could find someone who'd make me as happy as Luke makes Ash,' she said softly, 'I'd consider myself blessed.'

'Me, too,' Tom said. 'And the other way round. They're perfect for each other.'

'They certainly are,' she said with a smile, though at the same time there was a nagging ache in her heart. Would she ever find someone who'd make her happy, or was she always destined to date Mr Wrong?

Sean knew it was his duty—as the man who'd given the bride away—to dance with the chief bridesmaid at some point. For a second, he stood watching Claire as she danced with Luke's father. She was chatting away, looking totally at ease. And then Sean registered what the band was playing: 'Can't Take My Eyes Off You'. He was shocked to realise that it was true: he couldn't take his eyes off Claire.

Which was absolutely not a good thing.

Claire Stewart was the last woman he wanted to get involved with.

And yet he had to acknowledge that he was drawn to her. There was something about her.

He couldn't pin it down, which annoyed him even more—he couldn't put his feelings in a pigeonhole, the way he usually did. And that made her dangerous. He needed to stay well away from her.

Though, for tonight, he had to do the expected thing and make the best of it.

As the song came to an end, he walked over. 'I guess we need to play nice for Ashleigh.'

'I guess,' she said.

Even as the words came out of his mouth, he knew he was saying the wrong thing, but he couldn't stop himself asking, 'So is one of your awful boyfriends joining you later?'

'If that's your idea of nice,' Claire said, widening her eyes in what looked like annoyance, 'I'd hate to see how caustic your idea of snippy would be.'

He grimaced, knowing that he was in the wrong this time. 'Sorry. I shouldn't have put it quite like that.'

'Not if you were being nice. Though,' she said, 'I do admit that I have a terrible taste in men. I always seem to pick Mr Wrong.' She shrugged. 'And the answer's no, nobody's joining me. I'm happily single right now. And I'm way too busy at work right now to get involved with someone.'

Was that her way of telling him she wasn't

interested? Or was she just giving him the facts?

Her perfume wasn't one he recognised; it was something mysterious and deep. Maybe that was what was scrambling his brain, rather than her nearness. Scrambling his brain enough to make him think that she was the perfect fit. The way she felt, in his arms...

'So isn't one of your sweet-but-temporary girlfriends joining you later?' Claire asked.

Ouch. Though Sean knew he deserved the question. He'd started it. 'No. Becca and I broke up three months ago. And I'm busy at work.' Which was his usual excuse for ending a relationship before things started to get too close.

'Two peas in a pod, then, us,' she said with a grin.

'I always thought we were chalk and cheese.'

She laughed. 'I was going to say oil and vinegar. Except they actually go together.'

'And we don't,' Sean said. 'So would you be the vinegar or the oil?'

'Difficult to say. A bit of both, really,' she said. 'I make things go smoothly for my clients. But I'm sharp with people who have an attitude problem. You?'

'Ditto,' he said.

This was *weird*.

They were actually laughing at themselves. Together. Not sniping at each other.

And this felt sparky. Fun. He was actually enjoying Claire's company—something that he'd never thought would happen in a million years.

This was the second song in a row they were dancing to. The music was slower. Softer. And, although he knew it was a seriously bad idea, he found himself drawing Claire closer. Swaying with her.

Oh, help, Claire thought. She'd been here before. Today, she'd paced herself and only drunk a couple of small glasses of Prosecco, well spaced out with sparkling water. But she could still remember the first night she'd kissed Sean Farrell. The way his mouth had felt against hers before he'd pulled away and given her a total dressing-down about being seventeen years old and in a state where an unscrupulous man could've taken advantage of her.

And again, at Ashleigh and Luke's engagement party, where they'd ended up dancing way too close and then Sean had kissed her, his mouth warm and sweet and so tempting that it terrified her.

Right now, it would be all too easy to let her

hands drift up over his shoulders, curl round the nape of his neck, and draw his mouth down to hers. Particularly as they were no longer on the dance floor, in full view of the rest of the guests; at some point, while they'd been dancing together, they'd moved away from the temporary dance floor. Now they were in a secluded area of the garden. Just the two of them in the twilight.

'Claire.' His voice was a whisper.

And she knew he was going to kiss her again.

He dipped his head and brushed his mouth against hers, very lightly. It felt as if every nerve-end had been galvanised. He did it again. And again. This time, Claire gave in and slid her hands into his hair. His arms tightened round her and he continued teasing her mouth with those light, barely there kisses that made her want more. Maybe she made some needy little sound, because then he was really kissing her, and it felt as if fireworks were exploding all around them.

When he broke the kiss, she was shaking.

'Claire.' He sounded dazed.

That made two of them.

Part of her wanted to do this. To go with him—her room or his, it wouldn't matter. She knew they both needed a release from the tension of the last few days.

But the sensible part of her knew that doing that would make everything so much worse. How would they face each other in the morning? They certainly didn't have a future. Yes, Sean was reliable, unlike most of her past boyfriends—but he was also too regimented for her liking. Everything had to go within his twenty-year plan. Which was fine for a business, but it wasn't the way she wanted to live her personal life. She wanted to take time to smell the roses. Spontaneity. A chance to seize the day and enjoy whatever came her way. Live life to the full.

'We need to stop,' she said. While she could still be sensible. If he kissed her once more, she knew she'd say yes. So she'd say the word while she could still actually pronounce it. 'No.'

'No.' He looked at her, his eyes haunted. For a second, he looked so vulnerable. She was about to crack and place her palm against his cheek to comfort him, to tell him that she'd changed her mind, when she saw his expression change. His common sense had snapped back into place. 'You're absolutely right,' he said, and took a step back from her.

'I have bridesmaid stuff to do,' she said. It

wasn't strictly true—the rest of the evening was all organised—but it was an excuse that she thought would save face for both of them.

'Of course,' he said, and let her go.

Even as she walked away, Claire regretted it. Her old attraction to Sean had never quite gone away, no matter how deeply she thought she'd buried it or how much she denied it to herself.

But she knew it had been the right thing to do. Because no way could things work out between her and Sean, and she'd had enough of broken relationships and being let down. Keeping things platonic was sensible, and the best way to avoid heartbreak.

Claire spent the rest of the evening socialising with the other guests, encouraging the younger ones to dance. All the time, she was very aware of exactly where Sean was in the garden, but she didn't trust herself not to make another stupid mistake. She'd got it wrong with him in the past. She couldn't afford to get it wrong in the future.

Finally, she went back to the hotel with the last few guests, kicked off her high heels, and curled up in one of the wrought iron chairs on the balcony of her room, looking out at the moon's sparkling path on the sea. She'd been sitting there for a while when there was a knock at her door.

She wasn't expecting anyone, especially this late at night—unless maybe someone had been taken ill and needed help?

She padded over to the door, still in bare feet, and blinked in surprise when she saw Sean in the doorway. 'Is something wrong?'

'Yes,' he said.

She went cold. 'Ash?'

'No.'

Then she saw that he'd removed his jacket and cravat. He looked very slightly dishevelled, and it made him much more approachable. And much, much harder to resist.

He was also carrying a bottle of Prosecco and two glasses.

'Sean?' she asked, completely confused.

'I think we need to talk,' he said.

Again, for a split second, she glimpsed that vulnerability in his eyes. How could she turn him away when she had a good idea of how he was feeling—the same way she was feeling herself? 'Come in,' she said, and closed the door behind him.

'I saw you sitting on your balcony,' he said.

She nodded. 'I was a bit too wired to sleep, so I thought I'd look out over the sea and just chill for a bit.'

'Good plan.' He gestured to her balcony. 'Shall we?'

Sean, the sea and moonlight. A dangerous combination. It would be much more sensible to say no.

'Yes,' she said.

He uncorked the bottle with a minimum of fuss and without spilling a drop of the sparkling wine, then poured them both a glass.

Claire held hers up in a toast. 'To Ashleigh and Luke,' she said, 'and may they have every happiness in their life together.'

'Absolutely,' he said, clinking his glass against hers. 'To Ashleigh and Luke.'

'So you're too wired to sleep, too?' she asked.

He nodded. 'I was walking in the hotel gardens. That's when I saw you sitting on the balcony.'

'So why do we need to talk, Sean?'

He blew out a breath. 'You and me.'

The idea sent a shiver of pure desire through her.

'I think it's been a long time coming,' he said softly.

'But we don't even like each other. You think I'm a flake, and I think you're…well… a bit *too* organised,' she said, choosing her words carefully.

'Maybe,' he said, 'because it's easier for us to think that of each other.'

She took a sip of Prosecco, knowing that he was right but not quite wanting to admit it. 'You turned me down.'

'Nearly ten years ago? You know why,' he said. 'I think we've both grown up and got past that.'

'I guess.' She turned her glass round. 'Though I'm not in a hurry to put myself back in that situation.'

'You won't be,' he said softly. 'Because you're not seventeen any more, you're not drunk, and I'm not responsible for you.'

The three barriers that had been in the way, back then. It had hurt and embarrassed her at the time, but later Claire had appreciated how decent he'd been. Not that they'd ever discussed it. It was way too awkward for both of them.

But, now he'd said it, she needed to know. 'Back then, if I hadn't been drunk, if I'd been eighteen, and if you hadn't been responsible for me—would you have...?'

'Let you seduce me?' he asked.

She nodded.

His breath shuddered through him. 'Yes.'

Heat curled in her belly. That night, she'd wanted him so desperately. And, if the circumstances had been different, he would have made love with her. Been her first lover.

All the words were knocked out of her head. Because all she could think about was the way he'd kissed her tonight in the garden, and the way he looked right now. Sexy as hell.

'Ashleigh's engagement,' he said softly. '*You* turned *me* down, that time.'

'Because I was being sensible.' She paused. 'This isn't sensible, either.'

'I know. But your perfume's haunted me all evening,' he said, his voice low and husky and drenched in desire. 'Your mouth. And you've been driving me crazy in that dress.'

She made a last-ditch attempt at keeping the status quo. 'This is a perfectly demure bridesmaid's dress,' she said. 'It's down to my knees.'

'And I can't stop thinking about what you might be wearing under it.'

Her breath hitched. 'Can't you, now?'

The same heat that curled in her belly was reflected in his eyes. 'Going to show me?' he invited.

'We're on my balcony. Anyone could see us. *You* saw me,' she pointed out.

'Then maybe,' he said, 'we should go inside. Draw the curtains.'

She knew without a shadow of a doubt what was going to happen if they did.

There would be repercussions. Huge ones.

But the old desire had lanced sharply through her, to the point where she didn't care about the repercussions any more. 'Yes.'

Without a word, he stood up and scooped her out of her chair. Carried her into the room and set her down on her feet. He turned away just long enough to close the curtains, then pulled her into his arms and kissed her

That first kiss in the garden had been tentative, sweet. This was like lighting touchpaper, setting her on fire. By the time he broke the kiss, they were both shaking.

'Show me,' he said softly.

She reached behind her back to the zip and slid it down; then she held the dress to her.

He raised an eyebrow. 'Shy?'

She shook her head. 'I'm waiting for you to get rid of your waistcoat and undo your shirt.'

He looked puzzled, and she explained, 'Because, if we're going to do this, it's going to be equal. Both of us. All the way.'

'All the way,' Sean repeated huskily. He removed his waistcoat, then undid his shirt and pulled it out of the waistband of his trousers. 'Better?'

'Much better. It makes you look touchable,' she said.

'Good—because I want you to touch me, Claire. And I want to touch you.' He gestured to her dress. 'Show me.'

She felt ridiculously shy and almost chickened out; but then took a deep breath and stepped out of the dress before hanging it on the back of a chair.

'Now that I wasn't expecting—underwear to match your dress.' He closed the gap between them and traced the outline of her strapless lacy bra with the tip of his finger.

'I had it dyed at the same time as my shoes,' she said.

'Attention to detail—I like that,' he said approvingly.

She slid her palms against his pectoral muscles. 'Very nice,' she said, and let her hands slide down to his abdomen. 'A perfect six pack. I wasn't expecting that.'

'I don't spend the whole day in a chair. The gym gives me time to think about things,' he said.

'Good plan.' She slipped the soft cotton from his shoulders.

'So now I'm naked to the waist, and you're not. You said we were in this together, Claire.'

'Then do something about it,' she invited.

Sean smiled, unclipped her bra and let the lacy garment fall to the floor. Then scooped her up, carried her to the bed, and Claire stopped thinking.

CHAPTER FIVE

CLAIRE'S MOBILE SHRILLED. Still with her eyes closed, she groped for the phone on the bedside table. 'Hello?'

'C'mon, sleepyhead! You went to bed before I did—you can't *still* be snoozing,' Sammy said cheerfully. 'There's a pile of warm pastries and a bowl of freshly picked, juicy Italian peaches down here with our name on them. And the best coffee ever.'

Breakfast.

Claire had arranged to meet Sammy for breakfast.

And right now she was still in bed. *With Sean*. Whose arms were still wrapped round her, keeping her close.

'Uh—I'll be down as soon as I can,' Claire said hastily. 'If you're hungry, start without me.'

'Don't blame me if the pastries are all gone by the time you get here. See you soon,' Sammy said, her voice full of laughter.

'Who was that?' Sean asked when Claire put the phone down.

'Sammy. We arranged to have breakfast together this morning.' Claire dragged in a breath. 'Except...Sean, I...' She frowned. 'And now I'm being incoherent and stupid, and that isn't me.'

'Lack of sleep,' he said, nuzzling her shoulder. 'Which is as much my fault as yours.'

Oh, help. When he was being sweet and warm like this, it made her want what she knew she couldn't have. And she really had to be sensible about this. 'Sean—we really can't do this,' she blurted out.

'Do what?'

'Be together. Or let anyone know about what happened last night.' She twisted round to face him. 'You and me—you know it would never work out between us in a month of Sundays. We're too different. You have a twenty-year plan for everything, and I hate being boxed in like that. We'd drive each other bananas.'

'So, what? We're going to pretend last night didn't happen?' he asked.

'That'd probably be the best thing,' she said. 'Because then it won't be awkward when Ash asks us both over to see the wedding photos and what have you.'

'Uh-huh.' His face was expressionless.

And now she felt horrible. Last night had been a revelation about just how much attention Sean paid to things and how good he'd made her feel. And it had been better between them than she'd ever dreamed it would be as a starry-eyed teenager. If only they weren't so different, she'd be tempted to start a proper relationship with him. Seriously tempted. But she knew it wasn't going to work out between them, and she didn't want her oldest friendship to become collateral damage of a fling that didn't last. She swallowed hard. 'Last night… You made it good for me. Really good.'

'Dear John—it's not you, it's me,' he intoned, raising an eyebrow.

'It's both of us, and you know it,' she said. 'You hate the fact that I follow my heart. I know what you call me, Sean.' Just as she was pretty sure that he knew what she called him.

He shrugged. 'I guess you're right.'

So why did it make her feel so bad—so *guilty*? 'I'm not dumping you, and you're not dumping me, because we were never really together in the first place,' she said. 'We'd be a disaster as a couple.'

'Probably,' he agreed.

'Sammy's waiting for me downstairs. I don't get to see her that much, with her job taking her away so much. I promised her I'd be there. I really have to go,' Claire said, feeling even more awkward. She wanted to stay. She wanted to pretend that she and Sean were two completely different people and that it would have a chance of working out between them.

But she had to face the facts. Tomorrow they'd both be back in London. And no way could things work between them there. Their lives were too opposite, and they just wouldn't fit.

'I know I'm being rude and bratty and everything else, but would you mind, um, please closing your eyes while I grab some clothes and have the quickest shower in the world?' she asked.

'It's a little late for shyness,' he said dryly, 'given that we saw every millimetre of each other last night.'

Not just saw, either. The memory made her face hot. They'd touched. Stroked. Kissed.

'Even so,' she said.

'As you wish.' He rolled over and closed his eyes. 'Let me know when it's safe to look.'

'I'm sorry. I really wish things could be different,' she said, meaning it. 'But this is the best way. A clean break.'

'Apart from the fact that my little sister is your best friend, and we'll still have to see each other in the future.'

'And we'll do exactly the same as we've done for years and years,' she said. 'We'll be polite to each other for her sake, and avoid each other as much as we can.'

'Uh-huh.'

'Like you said, last night—well, it's been a long time coming. And now we've done it and it's out of our systems.' Which was a big, fat lie, so it was just as well that he couldn't see her face. She had a nasty feeling that Sean Farrell would never be completely out of her system. Especially now she knew what it was like to kiss him properly. To touch him. To make love with him.

She shook herself and grabbed some clothes. 'It's OK to look,' she said as she closed the bathroom door.

She showered and dressed in record time. When she walked back into the bedroom, Sean was already dressed and sitting on the bed, waiting for her. Well, he would. He had impeccable manners. 'Thank you,' she said. 'Um—I guess I'll see you in London when Ash gets back. And I'll sort out the money I owe you for that helicopter flight.'

Downstairs, Sammy was pouring a cup of coffee from a cafetière when Claire walked over to her table. 'So who was he?' she asked.

'Who was what?' Claire asked.

'The guy who kept you awake last night and gave you that hickey on the left-hand side of your neck.'

Claire clapped a hand to her neck and stared at her friend in utter dismay. She hadn't noticed a hickey while she was in the bathroom—well, not that she'd paid much attention to the mirror, because she'd been too busy panicking about the fact that Sean Farrell was naked and in her bed, and she'd just messed things up again.

And he'd given her a hickey?

Oh, no. She hadn't had a hickey since she was thirteen, and her dad had been so mad at her that she'd never repeated that particular mistake. Until now.

When Claire continued to be silent, Sammy laughed. 'Gotcha. There's no hickey. But clearly I wasn't far wrong and there *was* a guy last night.'

'You don't want to know,' Claire said.

'I wouldn't be fishing if I didn't,' Sammy pointed out.

'It was a one off. And I feel suitably ashamed, OK? I said I wouldn't date any more Mr Wrongs.'

'Forgive me for saying, but you didn't have a date for Ash's wedding,' Sammy said. 'So

I think he doesn't count as one of your Mr Wrongs.'

'Oh, he does. You couldn't get more wrong for me than him,' Claire said feelingly. More was the pity.

'Was the sex good?'

'Sammy!' Claire felt the colour hit her face like a tidal wave.

Her friend was totally unrepentant. 'Out of ten?'

Claire groaned. 'I need coffee.'

'Answer the question, Claire-bear.'

'Eleven,' Claire muttered, and helped herself to coffee, sugaring it liberally.

'Then maybe,' Sammy said, 'he might be worth working on. Sort out whatever makes him Mr Wrong.'

'That'd be several lifetimes' work,' Claire said wryly.

'Your call. Pastries or peaches?'

Claire couldn't help smiling. Only Sammy would ask something so outrageous followed by something so practical and mundane. 'I thought you'd already scoffed all the pastries? But if there are any left I'll have both,' she said.

'Attagirl.' Sammy winked at her. 'And I hope you don't have a hangover. Because we're taking that boat out to the Blue Grotto

this afternoon before we catch our flights—
I've got a commission.'

'Do you ever stop working?' Claire asked.

'About as much as you do,' Sammy said
with a grin. 'Anyway, mixing work and play
means you get to fit twice as much into your
day—and you enjoy it more.'

'True.'

'Pity about Mr Wrong.'

Yeah.

And Claire really wasn't looking forward
to facing Sean, the next time they met. Somehow, before then she needed to get her emotions completely under control.

Claire enjoyed her trip to the Blue Grotto, and
the colours and textures gave her several ideas
for future dress designs; but on the plane home
she found herself thinking about Sean. He'd
been a very focused lover, very considerate.
She still felt guilty about the way she'd called
a halt to it, but she knew she'd done the right
thing. Sean planned things out to the extreme,
and she preferred to follow her heart, so they'd
never be able to agree on anything.

Back at her flat, she unpacked and put the
laundry on, checked her mail and her messages, and made notes for what she needed to
do in the morning. Though she still couldn't

get Sean out of her head. When she finally fell asleep, she had the most graphic dream about him—one that left her hot and very bothered when her alarm went off on the Monday morning.

'Don't be so ridiculous. Sean Farrell is completely off limits,' she told herself firmly, and went for her usual pre-breakfast run. Maybe that would get her common sense back in working order. But even then she couldn't stop thinking about Sean. How he'd made her feel. How she wanted to do what they'd done all over again.

After her shower, she opened her laptop and logged in to her bank account so she could transfer the money she owed Sean for the flight into his account. And, once that was done, she knew she wouldn't need any contact with him until Ashleigh and Luke were back from honeymoon. By which time, her common sense would be back.

She hoped.

She went down to open the shop, then headed for her workroom at the back to start work on the next dress she needed to make for the wedding show. She'd just finished cutting it out when the old-fashioned bell on her door jangled to signal that someone was coming through the front door.

She came out from the workroom to see a delivery man carrying an enormous bunch of flowers. 'Miss Stewart?' he asked.

'Um, yes.'

'For you.' He smiled and handed her the flowers. 'Enjoy.'

'Thank you.'

It wasn't her birthday and she wasn't expecting any flowers. Or maybe they were from Ashleigh and Luke to say thanks for her help with the wedding. She absolutely loved dusky pink roses; the bouquet was stuffed with them, teamed with sweet-smelling cream freesias and clouds of fluffy gypsophila. She'd never seen such a gorgeous bouquet.

She opened the envelope that came with it and felt her eyes widen with shock; she recognised the strong, precise handwriting immediately, because she'd seen it on cards and notes at Ashleigh's flat over the years.

Saw these and thought of you. Sean.

He'd sent her flowers.

Not just any old flowers—glorious flowers.

And he hadn't just asked his PA to do it, either. The handwriting was his, so he'd clearly gone to the florist in person, and maybe even chosen the flowers himself.

Sean Farrell had sent her flowers.

Claire couldn't quite get her head round that.

Why would he send her flowers?

She didn't quite dare ring him to ask him. So, once she'd put them in water, she took the coward's way out and texted him.

Thank you for the flowers. They're gorgeous.

He took his time replying, but eventually the text came through. Glad you like them.

Where was he going with this?

Before she could work out a way to ask without sounding offensive, her phone beeped again to signal the arrival of another text.

Thank you for the flight money. Bank just notified me. Do you have an appointment over lunch?

Why? No, that sounded grudging and suspicious. She deleted the message and started again. No worries, and no, she typed back.

You do now. See you at your shop at one.

What? Was he suggesting a lunch date? Dating her? But—but—they'd agreed that the thing between them would be a disaster if they let it go any further.

Sean, we can't.

But he didn't reply. And she was left in a flat spin.

By the time the bell on the front door jangled and she went through to the shop to see Sean standing there—and he'd turned her sign on the door to 'closed', she noticed—she was wound up to fever pitch.

'What's this about, Sean?' she asked.

'I thought we could have lunch together.'

'But…' Her voice faded. They'd already agreed that this was a bad idea—hadn't they?

'I know,' he said softly, and walked over towards her.

He was dressed in another of his formal well-cut suits, with his shoes perfectly shined and his silk tie perfectly knotted; he was a million miles away from the sensual, dishevelled man who'd spent the night in her bed in Capri. And yet he was every bit as delectable. Even though he wasn't even touching her, being this close to him made all her senses go on red alert.

'I can't get you out of my head,' he said.

Well, if he could be brave enough to admit

it, so could she. She swallowed hard. 'Me, neither,' she said.

'So what do we do about this, Claire?' he asked. 'Because I have a feeling this isn't going away any time soon.'

'That night in Capri was supposed to—well—get it out of our systems,' she reminded him.

'And it didn't work,' he said. 'Not for me.'

His admission warmed her and terrified her at the same time.

'Claire?' he asked softly.

He deserved honesty. 'Me, neither.'

He leaned forward and brushed his lips against hers, ever so gently. And every nerve end on her mouth sizzled.

He tempted her. Oh, so much. But it all came back to collateral damage.

'We have to be sensible,' she said. 'And why am I the one saying this, not you? You're the one with—'

'—the twenty-year plan,' he finished. 'For the record, it's five years. Not twenty.'

'Even so. You have your whole life planned out.'

'There's nothing wrong with being responsible and organised,' he said.

'There's nothing wrong with being spontaneous, either,' she retorted.

He smiled. 'Not if it's like Saturday night, no.'

Oh, why had he had to bring that up again? Now her temperature was spiking. Seriously spiking. 'We're too different,' she said. 'You're my best friend's brother.'

'And?'

'There's a huge risk of collateral damage. I can't take that risk.' The risk of losing Ashleigh. Claire had already lost too much in her life. She wasn't prepared to risk losing her best friend as well. 'If it goes wrong between us. *When* it goes wrong between us,' she amended.

'Why are you so sure it will go wrong?'

That was an easy one. 'Because my relationships always go wrong.'

'Because you pick the kind of man who doesn't commit.'

She didn't have an answer to that. Mainly because she knew he was right.

'You pick men who say they're free spirits. And you think that'll work because you're a free spirit, too. Except,' he said softly, 'they always let you down.'

Claire thought of her last ex. The one who'd let her down so much that she'd temporarily sworn off relationships. He definitely hadn't been able to commit. She'd found him in bed with someone else—and then she'd discovered that he was cheating on both of them with yet *another* woman. Messy and a half.

And the worst thing was that he'd assumed she'd be OK with it, because she was a free spirit, too… It had been a wake-up call. Claire had promised herself that never again would she date someone who could be so casual with her feelings. But it had shaken her faith in her judgement of men. In a room full of eligible men, she was pretty sure she'd pick all the rotten ones.

'I guess,' she said. 'And anyway, what about you? You never date anyone for longer than three weeks.'

'It's not quite that bad.'

'Even so, that's not what I want, Sean. Three weeks and you're out. That's just…' She grimaced. 'No.'

'I'm always very clear with my girlfriends. That it's for fun, that I'm committed to the factory and won't have time to…' His voice faded.

'Actually, that makes you the kind of man who won't commit,' she said softly. 'Like every other man I date.'

Sean had never thought of himself in that way before. He'd thought of the way he conducted his relationships as protecting his heart. Not letting himself get too involved meant not risking losing someone. He'd already lost too much in his life, and he didn't want to lose any more. So he'd concentrated on his career rather than on his relationships. Because the business was *safe*. Staying in control of his emotions kept his heart safe.

'What do you want, Sean?' she asked.

Such an easy answer—and such a difficult one. Though he owed her honesty. 'You. I can't think beyond that at the moment,' he admitted. And that was scary. Claire had accused him of having a twenty-year plan; although it wasn't anywhere near that long-range, he had to admit that he always planned things out, ever since his parents had died and he'd taken over the family business.

Planning had helped him cope with being thrown in at the deep end and being responsible for everything, without having the safety net of his father's experience to help him. And planning meant that everything was always under control. Just the way he liked it.

She bit her lip. 'I've got a wedding show in two months. My first collection. This could make all the difference to my career—this could be what really launches me into the big time. I'm hoping that one of the big wedding fashion houses might give me a chance to work with them on a collection. So I really don't have time for a relationship right now.'

'And I've just finished fighting off a take-over bid from an international conglomerate who wanted to add Farrell's to their portfolio,' he said. 'The vultures are still circling. I need to concentrate on the business and make absolutely sure they don't get another opening. If anything, I need to expand and maybe float the company on the stock market to finance the expansion. It's going to take all my time and then some.'

'So we're agreed: this is the wrong time for either of us to start any kind of relationship. By the time it *is* the right time, we'll both be back to our senses and we'll know it'd be the wrong thing to do anyway.'

That was something else she'd thrown at him—he was the sensible one, the one who planned things out and was never spontaneous. So why wasn't he the one making this argument instead of her? Why had he sent her flowers and moved an appointment so he could see her for lunch?

It was totally crazy. Illogical.

And he couldn't do a thing to stop it.

Which exhilarated him and terrified him at the same time. With Claire, there was a real risk of losing control. And if he wasn't in control…what then? The possibilities made his head spin.

The only thing he could do now was to state the facts. 'I want you,' he said softly. 'And I think you want me.'

'So, what? We have a stupid, crazy, insane affair?'

He grimaced. 'Put like that, it sounds pretty sleazy.'

'But that's what you're offering.'

Was it? 'No.'

She frowned. 'So what *are* you suggesting, Sean?'

'I don't know,' he said. And it was a position he'd never actually been in before. He'd always been the one to call the shots. The one who initiated a relationship and the one who ended it. He shook his head, trying to clear it. But nothing changed. It was still that same spinning, out-of-control feeling. Like being on the highest, fastest, scariest fairground ride. 'All I know is that I want you,' he said.

'There's too much at stake. No.'

'Unless,' he said, 'we have an agreement.'

Her eyes narrowed. 'What kind of agreement?'

'We see each other. Explore where this thing goes. And then, whatever happens between us, we're polite to each other in front of Ashleigh. Nobody gets hurt. Especially her.'

'Can you guarantee that?' she asked softly.

'I can guarantee that I'll always be polite to you in front of Ashleigh.' He paused. 'The rest of it—I don't think anyone could guarantee that. But maybe it's worth the risk of finding out.' Risk. Something he didn't usually do unless it was precisely calculated. This wasn't calculated. At all. He needed his head examined.

'Maybe,' she said.

He curled his fingers round hers. His skin tingled where it touched her. 'Come and have lunch with me.'

She smiled then. Funny how it made the whole room light up. That wasn't something he was used to, either.

'OK,' she said. 'I just need to get my bag.'

'Sure.' He waited for her; then, when she'd locked the shop door behind them, he took her hand and walked down the street with her.

CHAPTER SIX

Claire was walking hand in hand with Sean Farrell. Down the high street in Camden. On an ordinary Monday lunchtime.

This was surreal, she thought.

And she couldn't quite get her head round it.

But his fingers were wrapped round hers, his skin was warm against hers, and it was definitely happening rather than being some kind of super-realistic dream—because when she surreptitiously pinched herself it hurt.

'So what do you normally do for lunch?' Claire asked.

'I grab a sandwich at my desk,' he said. 'In the office, we put an order in to a local sandwich shop first thing in the morning, and they deliver to us. You?'

'Pretty much the same, except obviously I eat it well away from my work area so I don't risk getting crumbs or grease on the material and ruining it,' she said.

'So we both work through lunch. Well, that's another thing we have in common.'

There was a gleam in his eye that reminded her of the first thing they had in common. That night in Capri. She went hot at the memory.

'So how long do you have to spare?' he asked.

'An hour, maybe,' she said.

'So that's enough time to walk down to Camden Lock, grab a sandwich, and sit by the canal while we eat,' he said.

'Sounds good to me.' The lock was one of her favourite places; even though the area got incredibly busy in the summer months, she loved watching the way the narrow boats floated calmly down the canal underneath the willow trees. 'But this is a bit strange,' she said.

'How?'

'I've been thinking—we've known each other for years, and I know hardly anything about you. Well, other than that you run Farrell's.' His family's confectionery business, which specialised in toffee.

'What do you want to know?' he asked.

'Everything. Except I don't know where to start,' she admitted. 'Maybe we should pretend we're speed-dating.'

He blinked. 'You've been speed-dating?'

'No. Sammy has, though. I helped her do a list of questions.'

'What, all the stuff about what you do, where you come from, that sort of thing?' At her nod, he said, 'But you already know all that.'

'There's other stuff as well. I think the list might still be on my phone,' she said.

'Let's grab some lunch, sit down and go through your list, then,' he said. 'And if we both answer the questions, that might be a good idea—now I think about it, I don't really know that much about you, either.'

She smiled wryly. 'I can't believe we're doing this. We don't even like each other.'

He glanced down at their joined hands. 'Though we're attracted to each other. And maybe we haven't given each other a proper chance.'

From Claire's point of view, Sean was the one who hadn't given her a chance; but she wasn't going to pick a fight with him over it. He was making an effort, and she'd agreed to see where this thing took them. It was exhilarating and scary, all at the same time. Exhilarating, because this was a step into the unknown; and scary, because it meant trusting her judgement again. Her track record where men were concerned was so terrible that...

No. She wasn't going to analyse this. Not now. She was going to see where this took them. Seize the day.

They walked down to Camden Lock, bought bagels and freshly squeezed orange juice from one of the stalls, and sat down on the edge of the canal, looking out at the narrow boats and the crowd.

Claire found the list on her phone. 'Ready?' she asked.

'Yup. And remember you're doing this, too,' he said.

'OK. Your favourite kind of book, movie and music?' she asked.

He thought about it. 'In order—crime, classic film noir and anything I can run to. You?'

'Jane Austen, rom-coms and anything I can sing to,' she said promptly.

'So we're not really compatible there,' he said.

She wrinkled her nose. 'We're not that far apart. I like reading crime novels, too, but I like historical ones rather than the super-gory contemporary stuff. And classic noir—well, if Jimmy Stewart's in it, I'll watch it. I love *Rear Window*.'

'I really can't stand Jane Austen. I had to do

Mansfield Park for A level, and that was more than enough for me,' he said with a grimace. 'But if the rom-com's witty and shot well, I can sit through it.'

She grinned. 'So you're a bit of a film snob, are you, Mr Farrell?'

He thought about it for a moment and grinned back. 'I guess I am.'

'OK. What do you do for fun?'

'You mean you actually think I might have fun?' he asked.

She smiled. 'You can be a little bit too organised, but I think there's more to you than meets the eye—so answer the question, Sean.'

'Abseiling,' he said, his face totally deadpan.

She stared at him, trying to imagine it—if he'd said squash or maybe even rugby, she might've believed him, but abseiling? 'In London?' she queried.

'There are lots of tall buildings in London.'

She thought about it a bit more, and shook her head. 'No, that's not you. I think you're teasing me.' Especially because he knew she was scared of heights.

'Good call,' he said. And his eyes actually *twinkled*.

Sean Farrell, teasing her. She would never

have believed that he had a sense of humour. 'So what's the real answer?' she asked.

'Something very regimented,' he said. 'Sudoku.'

'There's nothing wrong with doing puzzles,' she said. Though trust Sean to pick something logical.

'What about you? What do you do for fun?' he asked.

Given how he'd teased her, he really deserved this. She schooled her face into a serious expression. 'Shopping. Preferably for shoes.' Given what she did for a living, that would be totally plausible. 'Actually, I have three special shoe wardrobes. Walk-in ones.'

'Seriously?' He looked totally horrified.

'About as much as you go abseiling.' She laughed. 'I like shoes, but I'm not that extreme. No, for me it's cooking for friends and watching a good film and talking about it afterwards.'

'OK. We're even now,' he said with a smile. 'So what do you cook? Anything in particular?'

'Whatever catches my eye. I love magazines that have recipes in them, and it's probably one of my worst vices because I can never resist a news stand,' she said. 'What about you?'

'I can cook if I have to,' he said. 'Though I

admit I'm more likely to take someone out to dinner than to cook for them.'

She shrugged. 'That's not a big deal. It means you'll be doing the washing up, though.'

'Was that an offer?' he asked.

'Do you want it to be?' she fenced.

He held her gaze. 'Yes. Tell me when, and I'll bring the wine.'

There was a little flare of excitement in her stomach. They were actually doing this. Arranging a date. Seeing each other. She could maybe play a little hard to get and make him wait until Friday; but her mouth clearly had other ideas, because she found herself suggesting, 'Tonight?'

'I'd like that. I've got meetings until half past five, and some paperwork that needs doing after that—but I can be with you for seven, if that's OK?' he asked.

'It's a date,' she said softly.

He took her hand and brought it up to his mouth. Keeping eye contact all the way, he kissed the back of her hand, just briefly, before releasing it again; it made Claire feel warm and squidgy inside. Who would've thought that Sean Farrell was Prince Charming in disguise? Not that she was a weak little princess who needed rescuing—she could look after

herself perfectly well, thank you very much—
but she liked the charm. A lot.

'Next question,' he said.

'OK. What are you most proud of?' she
asked.

'That's an easy one—my sister and Farrell's,' he said.

His family, and his family business, she
thought. So it looked as if Sean Farrell had
a seriously soft centre, just like the caramel
chocolates his factory made along with the
toffee.

'How about you?' he asked.

'The letters I get from brides telling me how
much they loved their dress and how it really helped make their special day feel extra-
special,' she said.

'So you're actually as much of a workaholic
as you think I am?'

'Don't sound so surprised,' she said dryly.
'I know you see extreme things on a fashion catwalk and the pages of magazines, but
it doesn't mean that designers are all totally
flaky. I want my brides to feel really special
and that they look like a million dollars, in a
dress I've made just for them. And that means
listening to what their dream is, and coming
up with something that makes them feel their
dream's come true.'

'Having seen the dress you made for Ashleigh, I can understand exactly why they commission you,' he said. 'Next question?'

'What are you scared of?'

'Easy one. Anything happening to Ashleigh or the business.'

But he didn't meet her eye. There was clearly something else. Something he didn't want to discuss.

'You?' he asked.

'Heights. I'm OK in a plane, but chairlifts like that one in Capri make my palms go sweaty. Put it this way, I'm never, ever going skiing. Or abseiling.'

'Fair enough. Next?'

She glanced down at her phone to check. 'Your most treasured possession.'

'I can show you that.' He took his wallet out of his pocket, removed two photographs and handed them to her. One was of himself with Ashleigh, and the other was himself on graduation day with his parents on either side of him. Claire had a lump in her throat and couldn't say a word when she handed them back.

'You?' he asked.

'The same,' she whispered, and took her own wallet from her bag. She showed him a photograph of herself and her parents on her seventeenth birthday, and one of her with Ashleigh and Sammy and the Coliseum in the background.

He took her hand in silence and squeezed it briefly. Not that he needed any words; she knew he shared her feelings.

She put the photographs away. 'Next question—is the glass half full or half empty?'

'Half full. You?'

'Same,' she said, and glanced at her watch. 'We might have to cut this a bit short. Last one for now. Your perfect holiday?'

'Not a beach holiday,' he said feelingly. 'That just bores me silly.'

'You mean, you get a fit of the guilts at lying on a beach doing nothing, and you end up working.'

'Actually, I'm just not very good at just sitting still and doing nothing,' he admitted.

'So you'd rather have an active holiday?'

'Exploring somewhere, you mean?' He nodded. 'That'd work for me.'

'Culture or geography?'

'Either,' he said. 'I guess my perfect holiday would be Iceland. I'd love to walk up a volcano, and to see the hot springs and learn about the place. You?'

'I like city breaks. I have a bit of an art gallery habit, thanks to Sammy,' she explained.

'Plus I love museums where they have a big costume section. I should warn you that I really, really love Regency dresses. And I can spend hours in the costume section, looking at all the fine details.'

'So you see yourself as Lizzie Bennett?'

'No,' she said, 'and I'm not looking for a Darcy—anyway, seeing as you hate Austen, how come you know more than just the book you did for A level?'

'Ex-girlfriends who insisted on seeing certain films more than once, and became ex very shortly afterwards,' he said dryly.

'Hint duly noted,' she said. 'I won't ever ask you to watch *Pride and Prejudice* with me. Even though it's one of my favourite films.'

'Nicely skated past,' he said, 'but let's backtrack—you said you like holidays where you go and look at vintage clothes. And you said you look at details, so I bet you take notes and as many photos as you can get away with. Isn't that partly work?'

'Busted.' She clicked her fingers and grinned. 'I have to admit, I don't really like beach holidays, either. It's nice to have a day or two to unwind and read, but I'd rather see a bit of culture with friends. I really loved my trips in Italy with Ash and Sammy.'

'So what's your perfect holiday?' he asked.

'Anywhere with museums, galleries and lots of nice little places to eat. Philadelphia and Boston are next on my wish list.'

'This is scary,' he said. 'A week ago I would've said we were total opposites.'

She thought about it. 'We still are. We have a few things in common—probably more than either of us realised—but you like things really pinned down and I like to go with the flow.' She smiled. 'And I bet you have an itinerary on holiday. Down to the minute.'

'If you don't know the opening times and days for a museum or what have you, then you might go to see it when it's closed and not get a chance to go back,' he pointed out. 'So yes, I do have an itinerary.'

'But if you go with the flow, you discover things you wouldn't have known about otherwise,' she pointed out.

'Let's agree to disagree on that one.' He glanced at his watch. 'We'd better head back.'

'You don't have to walk me back, Sean. Go, if you have a meeting.'

'I was brought up properly. I'll walk you back,' he said.

'I'm planning a slight detour,' she warned.

He looked a little wary, but nodded. 'We'll do this your way, then.'

Her detour was to an ice cream shop where

the ice cream was cooled with liquid nitrogen rather than by being put in a freezer. 'I love this place. The way they make the ice cream is so cool,' she said, and laughed. 'Literally.'

'It's a little gimmicky,' he said.

'Just wait until you taste it.'

To her surprise, he chose the rich, dark chocolate. 'I would've pegged you as a vanilla man,' she said.

'Plain and boring?'

'Not necessarily. Seriously good vanilla ice cream is one of the best pleasures in the world—which is why I just ordered it.'

'True. But remember what I do for a living. And my favourite bit of my job is when I work with the R and D team. Am I really going to pass up chocolate?'

This was a side of Sean she'd never really seen. Teasing, bantering—*fun*. And she really, really liked that.

She watched him as he took a spoonful of ice cream. He rolled his eyes at her to signal that he thought she was overselling it. And then she saw his pupils widen.

'Well?' she asked.

'This is something else,' he admitted. 'I can forgive the gimmicky stuff. Good choice.'

'And if you hadn't gone with the flow, you

wouldn't have known the place was there.' She grinned. 'Admit it. I was right.'

'You were right about the ice cream being great. That's as far as I go.' He held her gaze. 'For now.'

It should've been cheesy and made her laugh at him. But his voice was low and sexy as hell, and there was the hint of a promise in his words that made her feel hot all over, despite the ice cream. It was enough to silence her, and she concentrated on eating her ice cream on the walk back to her shop.

'Well, Ms Stewart,' he said on her doorstep. 'I'll see you later. Though there is something you need to attend to.'

She frowned. 'What's that?'

'You have ice cream on the corner of your mouth.' Just as she was about to reach up and scrub it away, he stopped her. 'Let me deal with this.'

And then he kissed the smear of sweet confection away. Slowly. Sensually. By the time he'd finished, Claire was close to hyperventilating and her knees felt weak. Sean was kissing her *in the street*. This was totally un-Sean-like behaviour and it put her in a flat spin.

'Later,' he whispered, and left.

Although Claire spent the rest of the day

alternately talking to customers and working on the dress, in the back of her head she was panicking about what to cook for him. She had no idea what he liked. She could play safe and cook chicken—she was fairly sure that he wasn't a vegetarian. Wryly, she realised that this was when Sean's 'plan everything down to the last microsecond' approach would come in useful.

She could text him to check what he did and didn't like. But that meant doing it his way and planning instead of being spontaneous—and she didn't want to give him the opportunity to say 'I told you so'. Then again, she didn't want to cook a meal he'd hate, or something he was allergic to, so it would be better to swallow her pride.

She texted him swiftly.

Any food allergies I need to know about? Ditto total food hates.

The reply came back.

No and no. What's for dinner?

She felt safe enough to tease him.

Whatever I feel like cooking. Carpe diem.

When he didn't reply she wondered if she'd gone too far. Then again, he'd said that he was going to be in meetings all afternoon. She shrugged it off and concentrated on making the dress she'd cut out that morning.

Though by the end of the afternoon she still hadn't decided what to cook. She ended up having a mad dash round the supermarket and picked up chicken, parma ham, asparagus and soft cheese so she could make chicken stuffed with asparagus, served with tiny new potatoes, baby carrots and tenderstem broccoli.

Given that Sean was a self-confessed chocolate fiend, she bought the pudding rather than making it from scratch—tiny pots of chocolate ganache, which she planned to serve with raspberries, as their tartness would be a good foil to the richness of the chocolate.

Once she'd prepared dinner, she fussed around the flat, making sure everywhere was tidy and all the important surfaces were gleaming. Then she changed her outfit three times, and was cross with herself for doing so. Why was she making such a big deal out of this? She'd known Sean for years. He'd seen her when she had teenage spotty skin and chubby cheeks. And this was her flat. It shouldn't matter what she wore. Jeans and a strappy vest top would be fine.

Except they didn't feel fine. Sean was always so pristine that she'd feel scruffy.

In the end, she compromised with a little black dress but minimal make-up and with her hair tied back. So he'd know that she'd made a little more effort than just dragging on a pair of jeans and doing nothing with her hair, but not so much effort that she was making a big deal out of it.

The doorbell rang at seven precisely—exactly what she'd expected from Sean, because of course he wouldn't be a minute late or a minute early—and anticipation sparkled through her.

Dinner.

And who knew what else the evening would bring?

CHAPTER SEVEN

HE WAS ACTUALLY *NERVOUS*, Sean realised.

Which was crazy.

This was Claire. He'd known her for years. There was nothing to be nervous about. Except for the fact that this was a date, and in the past they'd never really got on. And the fact that, now he was getting to know her, he was beginning to realise that maybe she wasn't the person he'd thought she was.

Would it be the same for her? He had no idea.

He took a deep breath and rang the doorbell.

When she opened the door, she was barefoot and wearing a little black dress, and her hair was tied back at the nape with a hot pink chiffon scarf. He wanted to kiss her hello, but was afraid he wouldn't be able to stop himself—it had been tough enough to walk away at lunchtime. So instead he smiled awkwardly at her. 'Hi. I wasn't sure what to bring, so I brought red and white.'

'You really didn't need to, but thank you very much.' She accepted the bottles with a smile. 'Come up.'

She looked so cool, unflustered and so-phisticated. Sean was pretty sure that she wasn't in the slightest bit nervous, and in turn that made him relax. This was just dinner, the getting-to-know-you stuff. And he really should stop thinking about how easy it would be to untie that scarf and let her glorious hair fall over her shoulders, then kiss her until they were both dizzy.

He followed her up the stairs and she ushered him in to the kitchen.

'We're eating in here, if that's OK,' she said. 'Can I get you a drink? Dinner will be ten minutes.'

'A glass of cold water would be fabulous, thanks.' At her raised eyebrows, he explained, 'It's been a boiling hot day and I could really do with something cold and non-alcoholic.'

'Sure.' She busied herself getting a glass and filled it from the filter jug in the fridge, adding ice and a frozen slice of lime. When she handed the glass to him, her fingers brushed against his; it sent a delicious shiver all the way down his spine.

Her kitchen was a place of extremes. The work surfaces had all been used, and it looked as if most of her kitchen equipment had been piled up next to the sink. The fridge was covered with magnets and photos, and a cork board on one wall had various cards and notes pinned to it, along with what looked like a note of a library fine. Chaos. And yet the bistro table was neatly set for two, and there was a compact electric steamer on the worktop next to the cooker, containing the vegetables. So there was a little order among the chaos.

Much like Claire herself.

'Something smells nice,' he said.

'Dinner, I hope,' she said, putting the white wine into the fridge.

He handed her a box. 'I thought these might be nice with coffee after dinner.'

'Thank you.' She smiled. 'Toffee, I assume?'

'Samples,' he said, smiling back. 'There have to be some perks when you're dating a confectioner.'

'Perks. Hmm. I like the sound of that, though if we're talking about a lot of calories here then I might have to start doubling the length of my morning run.' She did a cute wrinkly thing with her nose that made his knees go weak, then looked in the box. 'Oh, you brought those lovely soft caramel hearts! Fabulous. Thank you.'

Clearly she liked those; he made a mental note, and hoped she wouldn't be disappointed with what these actually were. 'Not *quite*,' he said.

'What are they, then?'

'Wait until coffee. Is there anything I can do to help?'

'No, you're fine—have a seat.' She gestured to the bistro table, and he sat down on one of the ladder-back chairs.

Small talk wasn't something Sean was used to doing with Claire, and he really wasn't sure what to say. It didn't help that he was itching to kiss her; but she was bustling round the kitchen, and he didn't want to distract her and ruin the effort she'd put into making dinner. 'It's a nice flat,' he said.

She nodded. 'I like it here. The neighbours are lovely, the road's quiet, and yet I'm five minutes away from all the shops and market stalls.'

Work. An excellent subject, he thought. They could talk about that. 'So how did the dressmaking go today? Are you on schedule for your big show?'

'Fine, thanks, and I think I am. How about your meetings?'

'Fine, thanks.' Then it finally clicked that she wasn't as cool and calm as she seemed.

She was being super-polite. So did that mean that she felt as nervous about this as he did? 'Claire, relax,' he said softly.

'Uh-huh.' But she still looked fidgety, and he noticed that she didn't sit down with him. Was she just feeling a little shy and awkward because of the newness of their situation, or was she having second thoughts?

'Have you changed your mind about this?' he asked, as gently as he could.

'No-o,' she hedged. 'It's not that.'

'What is it, then?'

'I'm usually a reasonable cook.' She bit her lip. 'What if it all goes wrong tonight?'

Nervous, then, rather than second thoughts. And suddenly his own nerves vanished. He stood up, walked over to her and put his arms round her. 'I'm pretty sure it'll be just fine. If it's not, then it doesn't matter. I'll carry you to your bed and take your mind off it—and then I'll order us a pizza instead.' He kissed the corner of her mouth, knowing he was dangerously close to distracting her, but wanting to make her feel better. 'Claire, why are you worrying that the food's going to be bad tonight?'

'Because it's *you*,' she said.

Because she thought he'd judge her? He had to acknowledge that he'd judged her in the past—and not always fairly. 'You already know I'd rather wash up or take someone out to dinner than cook for them, so I'm in no position to complain if someone cooks me something that isn't Michelin-star standard.'

'I guess.' She blew out a breath. 'It's just... Well, this is you and me, and it feels...'

He waited. What was she going to say? That it felt like a mistake?

'Scary,' she finished.

He could understand that. Claire fascinated him; yet, at the same time, this whole thing scared him witless. Her outlook was so different from his. She didn't have a totally ordered world. She followed her heart. If he let her close—what then? Would he end up with his heart broken? 'Me, too,' he said.

The only thing he could do then was to kiss her, to stop the fear spreading through him, too. So he covered her mouth with his, relaxing as she wrapped her arms round him, too, and kissed him back. Holding her close, feeling the warmth of her body against his and the sweetness of her mouth against his, made his world feel as if the axis was in the right place again.

A sharp ding made them both break apart. 'That was the steamer. It means the vegetables are done,' Claire said, looking flustered and adorably pink.

'Is there anything I can do to help?' he asked again.

This time, to his relief, she stopped treating him like a guest who had to be waited on. 'Could you open the wine? The corkscrew's in the middle drawer.'

'Sure. Would you prefer red or white?'

'We're having chicken, so it's entirely up to you.'

He looked at her. 'You'd serve red wine with chicken?'

'Well, hey—if you can cook chicken in red wine, then you can serve it with red wine.'

He wrinkled his nose at her. 'Am I being regimented again?'

'No. Just a teensy bit of a wine snob,' she said with a grin. 'You need to learn to go with the flow, Sean. *Carpe diem.* Seize the day. It's a good motto to live by.'

'Maybe.' By the time he'd taken the wine from her fridge, found the corkscrew in the jumble of her kitchen drawer, uncorked the bottle and poured them both a glass, she'd served up.

He sat down opposite her and raised his glass. 'To us, and whatever the future might bring.'

'To us,' she echoed softly, looking worried and uncertain—vulnerable, even—and again he felt that weird surge of protectiveness towards her. It unsettled him, because he didn't generally feel like that about his girlfriends.

'This is really lovely,' he said after his first mouthful. Chicken, stuffed with soft cheese and asparagus, then wrapped in parma ham. Claire Stewart was definitely capable in the kitchen, and he could tell that this had been cooked from scratch. He'd assumed that she'd be the sort to buy ready-made meals from the supermarket; clearly that wasn't the case.

'Thank you.' She acknowledged his compliment with a smile.

'But you're not reasonable.'

She frowned. 'Excuse me?'

'You called yourself a reasonable cook,' he said. 'You're not. You're more than that.'

'Thank you. Though I wasn't fishing for compliments.' She shrugged. 'I used to like cooking with my mum. Not that she ever followed a recipe. She'd pick something at random, and then she'd tweak it.'

'So I'm guessing that you didn't follow a recipe for this, did you?' he asked.

'I cooked us dinner. It's not exactly rocket science,' she drawled.

Why had he never noticed how deliciously sarcastic she could be?

'What?' she asked

He blinked. 'Sorry. I'm not following you.'

'You were smiling. What did I say that was so funny?'

'It was the way you said it.' He paused. 'Do you have any idea how delectable you are when you're being sarcastic?'

It was her turn to blink. 'Sarcasm is sexy?'

'It is on you.'

She grinned. 'Well, now. I think tonight has just got a whole lot more interesting. Are you on a sugar rush, Sean?'

'Excuse me?'

'Working where you do, you have toffee practically on tap. Eat enough of the stuff and you'll be on a permanent sugar rush. Which, I think, must be the main reason why you're complimenting me like this tonight.'

No. It was because it was as if he'd just met her for the first time. She wasn't the girl who'd irritated him for years; she was a woman who intrigued him. But he didn't want to sound soppy. 'Honey,' he drawled, 'the only sugar I want right now is you.'

She laughed at him. 'Now you've switched to cheese.'

'No. You're the one who's served cheese.'

He indicated the stuffing for the chicken. 'And very nice it is, too.'

Her mouth quirked. 'Keep complimenting me like this, and...'

'Yeah?' he asked, his voice suddenly lower. What was she going to do? Kiss him? That idea definitely worked for him.

'Oh, shut up and eat your dinner,' she said, looking flustered.

'Chicken,' he said, knowing that she'd pick up on the double use of the word—and he was seriously enjoying fencing with her. Why had he never noticed before that she was bright and funny, and sexy as hell?

Probably because he'd had this fixed idea of her as a difficult girl who attracted trouble. That was definitely true in the past, but now... Now, she wasn't who he'd always thought she was. She'd grown up. Changed. And he really liked the woman he was beginning to get to know.

She served pudding next—a seriously rich chocolate ganache teamed with tart raspberries. 'Come and work for my R and D department,' he said, 'because I think you'd have seriously good ideas about flavouring.'

She smiled. 'I know practically nothing about making toffee, and if I make banoffee pie I always buy a jar of *dulce de leche* rather than making my own.'

'That's a perfectly sensible use of your time,' he said.

She grinned. 'It's not so much that you have to boil a can of condensed milk for a couple of hours and keep an eye on it.'

'What, then?'

'I had a friend who tried doing it,' she explained. 'The can exploded and totally wrecked her kitchen.'

'Ouch.' He grimaced in sympathy, and took another spoonful of pudding. 'This is a really gorgeous meal, Claire.'

'I didn't make the ganache myself—it's a shop-bought pudding.'

'I don't care. It's still gorgeous. And I appreciate the effort. Though, for future reference, you could've ordered in pizza and I would've been perfectly happy,' he said. 'I just wanted to spend time with you.'

'Me, too,' she said softly. 'But I wanted to—well…'

Prove to him that she wasn't the flake he'd always thought she was? 'I know. And you did.'

And how weird it was that he could follow the way she thought. Scary, even. She was the last woman in the world he'd expected to be so in tune with.

Once he'd helped her clear away, she said, 'I thought we could have coffee in the living room.'

'Sounds good to me.'

'OK. You can go through and put on some music, if you like,' she suggested.

Claire's living room had clearly been hastily tidied, judging by the edges of the magazines peeking from the side of her sofa—he remembered her telling him that she was addicted to magazines; but the flowers he'd sent her that morning were in a vase on the coffee table, perfectly arranged. Clearly she liked them and hadn't just been polite when she'd thanked him for them earlier. And, given the pink tones in the room, he'd managed to pick her favourite colours.

Her MP3 player was in a speaker dock. He took it out and skimmed through the tracks. Given what she'd said at lunchtime, he'd expected most of the music to be pop, but he was surprised to see how much of it was from the nineteen-sixties. In the end, he picked a general compilation and switched on the music.

She smiled when she came in. 'Good choice. I love the Ronettes.' She sang a snatch of the next line.

'Aren't you a bit young to like this stuff?' he asked.

'Nope. It's the sort of stuff my gran listens to, so I grew up with it—singing into hairbrushes, the lot,' she said with a smile. 'Best Friday nights ever. Totally girly. Me, Mum, Gran, Aunt Lou and my cousins. Popcorn, waffles, milkshake and music.'

It was the first time she'd talked about her family. 'So you're close to your family?' he asked.

'Yes. I still clash quite a bit with my dad,' she said, 'but that's hardly tactful to talk about that to you.'

'Because I'm male?'

'Because,' she said softly, 'I'd guess that, like Ash, you'd give anything to be able to talk to your dad. And here am I grumbling about my remaining parent. Though, to be fair, my dad is nothing like yours was. Yours actually *listened*.'

Fair point. He did miss his parents. And, when the whole takeover bid had kicked off, Sean would've given anything to be able to talk about it to his dad. But at the same time he knew that relationships were complicated. And it was none of his business. Unless Claire wanted to talk about it, he had to leave the subject alone.

She'd brought in a tray with a cafetière, two mugs, a small jug of milk and the box he'd given her earlier. 'Milk and sugar?' she asked.

'Neither, thanks. I like my caffeine unadulterated,' he said with a smile.

Claire, he noticed, took hers with two sugars and a lot of milk. Revolting. And it also made him worry that she wouldn't like the samples he'd brought; she probably preferred white chocolate to dark. Then again, he'd been wrong about a lot of things where Claire was concerned.

'Right. This box of utter yumminess. Whatever else I might have said about you in the past,' she said, 'I've always said that you make seriously good toffee.'

Honesty compelled him to say, 'No, my staff do. I'm not really hands-on in the manufacturing department.'

'Now that surprises me,' she said. 'I would've pegged you as the kind of manager who did every single job in the factory so you knew exactly what all the issues are.'

'I have done, over the years,' he said. 'Everything from the manufacturing to packing the goods, to carrying the boxes out for delivery. And every single admin role. And, yes, I worked with the cleaning team as well. Nowadays, I have regular meetings with each department and my staff know that I want to know about any problems they have and can't smooth out on their own.'

'Attention to detail.'

Her voice sounded almost like a purr. And there was a suspicious glow of colour across her cheeks.

'Claire?'

'Um,' she said. 'Just thinking. About Capri. About…'

And now he was feeling the same rush of blood to the head. 'Close your eyes,' he said.

Her breathing went shallow. 'Why?'

'Humour me?'

'OK.' She closed her eyes.

He took one of the dark salted caramel chocolates from the box and brushed it against her lips. Her mouth parted—and so did the lashes on her left eye.

'No peeking,' he said.

In return, she gave him an insolent smile and opened both eyes properly. 'So we're playing, are we, Mr Farrell?'

'We are indeed, Ms Stewart. Now close your eyes.' He teased her mouth with the chocolate and made her reach for it before finally letting her take a bite.

'You,' she said when she'd eaten it, 'have just

upped your game considerably. I love the caramel-filled hearts, but these are spectacular.'

'You liked them?' Funny how that made him feel so good.

'Actually, I think I need another one, to check.'

He laughed. 'Oh, really?'

'Yes, really.' She struck a pose.

No way was he teasing her with chocolate when she looked like that, all pouting and dimpled and sexy as hell. Instead, he leaned over and kissed her.

The next thing he knew, they were both lying full length on the sofa and she was on top of him, his arms were wrapped tightly round her, and one of his hands was resting on the curve of her bottom.

'You're telling me that was chocolate?' she deadpanned.

'Maybe. Maybe not.' He moved his hand, liking the softness of her curves. 'Claire. You're...'

'What?'

'Unexpectedly luscious,' he said. 'None of this was supposed to happen.'

'Says the man who made me close my eyes and lean forward to take a bite of chocolate. Giving him a view straight down the front of my dress, if I'm not mistaken.'

'It was a very nice view,' he said, and shifted slightly so she was left in no doubt of his arousal.

'This is what chocolate does to you?' she asked.

'No. This is what *you* do to me.'

She leaned forward and caught his lower lip between hers, teasing him. 'Indeed, Mr Farrell.'

'Yeah.' He was aware that his voice sounded husky. She'd know from that exactly how much she affected him.

'So did you come prepared?' she asked.

He couldn't speak for a moment. And then he looked into her eyes. 'Are you suggesting…?'

'Capri, redux?' She held his gaze and nodded.

He blew out a breath. 'I didn't come prepared.'

'Tsk. Not what I expected from Mr Plan-Everything-Twenty-Years-in-Advance,' she teased.

'How do you manage to do that?' he asked plaintively.

'Do what?'

'Make me feel incredibly frustrated and make me want to laugh, all at the same time?'

'Go with the flow, sweetie,' she drawled.

He kissed her again. 'OK. Tonight wasn't about expectations. It wasn't about sending you flowers this morning so you'd sleep with me tonight. It was about getting to know you better.'

'Platonic, you mean?'

'I'd like to be friends.'

'Uh-huh.' She sounded unaffected, but he'd seen that little vulnerable flicker in her expression and he didn't let her move. He pulled her closer.

'I didn't say *just* friends. I want to be your lover as well.'

Her pupils went gratifyingly large.

'But I didn't come prepared because I'm not taking you for granted.'

To his surprise, he saw a sheen of tears in her eyes. 'Claire? What's wrong?'

She shook her head. 'I'm being wet.'

'Tell me anyway.'

'That's not how it usually is, for me,' she admitted.

Not being taken for granted? He brushed his mouth very gently against hers. 'That's because you've been dating the wrong men, thinking they're Mr Right.'

'I always thought you'd be Mr Wrong,' she admitted.

'And I always thought you'd be Ms Wrong,'

he said. 'But maybe we should give each other a little more of a chance.'

'Maybe,' she said softly. 'But next time—I think I'm going to be prepared.'

'You and me, both.' He nuzzled the curve of her neck. 'Careful, Claire. You might turn into a bit of an *über*-planner if you keep this up.'

As he'd hoped, she laughed. 'And you might start going with the flow without having to be reminded.'

He laughed back. 'I think we need to move. While we still both have some self-control.'

'Good plan.' But when she climbed off him, he didn't let her move away and sit in a different chair. He kept hold of her hand and drew her down beside him.

'This works for me,' he said. 'Just simply holding hands with you.'

For a moment, she went all dreamy-eyed. 'Like teenagers.'

'What?'

She shook her head. 'Ah, no. I'm not confessing that right now.'

Confessing what? He was intrigued. 'I could,' he suggested sweetly, '*make* you confess. Remember, I'm armed with seriously good chocolate.'

She drew his hand up to her mouth and kissed each knuckle in turn. 'But I also happen to know you're a gentleman. So you won't push me right now.'

So even when she hadn't liked him, she'd recognised that he had integrity and standards and knew that she was safe with him? That warmed him from the inside out. 'I won't push you right now,' he agreed. He handed her the box. 'Help yourself.'

'Salted caramel in dark chocolate. Fabulous. Are they all like that?'

'No. There's a Seville orange version and an espresso.'

'Nice choices. And you said earlier they were samples.' She looked thoughtful. 'So are you experimenting with new lines?'

'Possibly.'

She rolled her eyes. 'Sean, I'm hardly going to rush straight off to one of your competitors and sell them the information.'

'Of course you're not.' He frowned. 'Do you think I'm that suspicious?'

'You sounded it,' she pointed out.

'It's an experiment, moving into a slightly different form of toffee,' he said, 'but I need to put them through some focus groups first and see what my market thinks.'

'Ah, research. Looking at growing your market share.' She smiled. 'So either you sell the same product to more people, or you sell more products to the same people.'

At his raised eyebrow, she sighed. 'I'm not a total dimwit, you know. I've had my own business for three years.'

'I know, and it's not just that. Ashleigh told me you turned down an unconditional offer from Cambridge for medicine, and I know you wouldn't get that sort of offer if you weren't really bright.' He looked at her. 'I always wondered why you became a wedding dress designer instead of a doctor.'

She looked sad. 'It's a long story, and I don't really want to tell it tonight.'

Because she didn't trust him not to judge her? 'Fair enough,' he said coolly.

'I wasn't pushing you away, Sean,' she said. 'I just don't want to talk about it right now.'

'So what do you want, Claire?' He couldn't resist the question.

'Right now? I want you to kiss me again. But we've both agreed that's, um, possibly not a good idea.'

'Because I'm not prepared, and neither are you. So we'll take a rain check,' he said.

'How long?' She slapped a hand to her forehead. 'No. I didn't ask that and you didn't hear me.'

'Right. And I wasn't thinking it, either,' he retorted. 'When?'

'Wednesday?'

Giving them two days to come to their common sense. 'Wednesday,' he agreed. 'I would offer to cook for you, except you'd get a sandwich at best.'

She laughed. 'I can live with sandwiches.'

'No, I mean a proper date.'

'Planned to the nth degree, Sean-style?' she asked.

Why did planning things rattle her so much? In answer, he kissed her. Hard. And she was breathless by the time she'd finished.

'That was cheating,' she protested.

'Yeah, yeah.' He rubbed the pad of his thumb along her lower lip. 'And?'

'Go home, Sean, before we do something stupid.'

'Rain check,' he said. 'Wednesday night. I'll pick you up at seven.' He leaned forward and whispered in her ear, 'And, by the time I've finished with you, you won't remember what your name is or where you are.'

Her voice was gratifyingly husky when she said, 'That had better be a promise.'

'It is.' He stole one last kiss. 'And I always keep my promises. Which reminds me—I have washing-up duties.'

'I'll let you off,' she said.

'The deal was, you'd cook and I'd wash up.'

'Do you really think it's a good idea for us to be that close to each other, in the presence of water, and while neither of us is, um, prepared?'

He didn't quite get the reference to water, but he agreed with the rest of it. 'Good point. Rain check on the washing up, then, too?'

She laughed. 'No need. I have a dishwasher. It's horribly indulgent, given that I live on my own, but it's nice when I have friends over for dinner.' She paused, and added in a softer, sexier, deeper tone, 'Or my lover.'

Which sounded as if she was going to invite him back.

And that set his pulse thrumming.

'Right.' He couldn't resist one last kiss, one that sent his head spinning and left her looking equally dazed. 'Enjoy the chocolate,' he said. And then he left, while he was still capable of being sensible.

CHAPTER EIGHT

Sean sent Claire a text later that evening.

Sweet dreams.

Yes, she thought, because they'd be of him. She typed back, You, too x.

He'd turned out to be unexpectedly sweet, so different from how he'd always been in the past. He was still a little regimented, but there was huge potential for him to be…

She stopped herself. No. This time she wasn't going to make the same old mistake. She wasn't going into this relationship thinking that Sean might be The One, that there would definitely be a happy-ever-after. OK, so he wasn't like the men she usually dated; but that didn't guarantee a different outcome for this relationship, either.

And this was early days. Sean had a reputation for not dating women for very long;

the chances were, this would all be over in another month. Claire knew that she needed to minimise the potential damage to her heart and make sure that her best friend didn't get caught in any crossfire. Which meant keeping just a little bit of distance between them.

Even though Claire tried to tell herself to be sensible, she still found herself anticipating Wednesday. Wondering if he'd kiss her again. Wondering if they'd end up at his place or hers. Wondering if this whole thing blew his mind as much as it did hers.

Wednesday turned out to be madly busy, and Claire spent a long time on the phone with one of her suppliers, sorting out a mistake they'd made in delivering the wrong fabric—and it was going to cost her time she didn't have. A last-minute panic from one of her brides took up another hour; and, before she realised it, the time was half past six.

Oh, no. She still needed to shower, wash her hair, change and do her make-up before Sean arrived. She called him, hoping to beg an extra half an hour, but his line was busy. Swiftly, she tapped in a text as she went up the stairs to her flat.

Sorry, running a bit late. See you at half-seven?

She pressed 'send' and dropped the phone on her bed before rummaging through her wardrobe to find her navy linen dress.

She'd just stepped out of the shower and wrapped a towel round her hair when her doorbell rang.

No. It couldn't be Sean. It couldn't be seven-thirty already.

Well, whoever it was would just have to call back another time.

The bell rang again.

Arrgh. Clearly whoever it was had no intention of being put off. If it was a cold-caller, she'd explain firmly and politely that she didn't buy on the doorstep.

She blinked in surprise when she opened the door to Sean. 'You're early!' And Sean was never early and never late; he was always precisely on time.

'No. We said seven.'

She frowned. 'But I texted you to say I was running late and asked if we could make it half past.'

'I didn't get any text from you,' he said.

'Oh, no. I'm so sorry.' She blew out a breath. 'Um, come up. I'll be twenty minutes, tops— make yourself a coffee or something.'

'Do you want me to make you a drink?'

She shook her head. 'I'm so sorry.'

He stole a kiss. 'Stop apologising.'

'I'll be as quick as I can,' she said, feeling horribly guilty. Why hadn't she kept a better eye on the time? Or called him rather than relying on a text getting through?

She had to dry her hair roughly and tie it back rather than spending time on a sophisticated updo, but she was ready by twenty-five past seven.

'You look lovely,' he said.

'Thank you.' Though she noticed that he'd glanced at his watch again. If only he'd lighten up a bit. It would drive her crazy if he ran this evening to schedule, as if it were a business meeting. 'Where are we going?' she asked brightly.

'South Bank.'

'Great. We can play in the fountains,' she said with a smile. 'It's been so hot today that it'd be nice to have a chance to cool down.'

He simply glanced at his suit.

And she supposed he had a point. Getting soaked wouldn't do the fabric any favours. Or her dress, for that matter. But the art installations on the South Bank were *fun*.

'I called the restaurant to say we'd be late,' he said.

Sean and his schedules. Though if they didn't turn up when they were expected, the restaurant would be perfectly justified in giving their table to someone else, so she guessed it was reasonable of him. 'Sorry,' she said again.

This was the side of Sean she found harder to handle. Mr Organised. It was fine for business; but, in his personal life, surely he could be more relaxed?

They caught the tube to the South Bank—to her relief, the line was running without any delays—and the restaurant turned out to be fabulous. Their table had a great view of the river, and the food was as excellent as the view. Claire loved the fresh tuna with mango chilli salsa. 'And the pudding menu's to die for,' she said gleefully. 'It's going to take me ages to choose.'

'Actually, we don't have time,' Sean said, looking at his watch,

'No time for pudding? But that's the best bit of dinner out,' she protested.

'We have to be somewhere. Maybe we can fit pudding in afterwards,' he said.

Just as she'd feared, Sean had scheduled this evening down to the last second. If she hadn't been running late in the first place, it might not have been so much of a problem. But right now she was having huge second thoughts about dating Sean. OK, so he managed to fit a lot in to his life; but all this regimentation drove her crazy. They were too different for this to work.

'So why exactly do we have to rush off?' she asked.

'For the next bit of this evening,' he said.

'Which is?'

'A surprise.'

Half past eight was too late for a theatre performance to start, and if they'd been going to the cinema she thought he would probably have picked a restaurant nearer to Leicester Square. She didn't work out what he'd planned until they started walking towards the London Eye. 'Oh. An evening flight.'

'It's the last one they run on a weeknight,' he confirmed. 'And we have to pick up the tickets fifteen minutes beforehand. Sorry I rushed you through dinner.'

At least he'd acknowledged that he'd rushed her. And she needed to acknowledge her part in the fiasco. 'If I hadn't been running late, you wouldn't have had to rush me.' She bit her lip. 'I'm beginning to think you might be right about me being chaotic. I should've checked that the text had gone or left you a voicemail as well.'

'It's OK. Obviously you had a busy day.'

She nodded. 'There were a couple of glitches

that took time to sort out,' she said. 'And I'm up to my eyes in the wedding show stuff.'

'It'll be worth it in the end,' he said.

'I hope so. And I had a new bride in to see me this morning. That's my favourite bit of my job,' Claire said. 'Turning a bride-to-be's dreams into a dress that will suit her and make her feel special.'

'That's why you called your business "Dream of a Dress", then?' he asked.

'Half of the reason, yes.'

'And the other half?' he asked softly.

'Because it's my dream job,' she said.

He looked surprised, as if he'd never thought of it that way before. 'OK. But what if a bride wants a dress that you know wouldn't suit her?'

'You mean, like a fishtail dress when she's short and curvy?' At his nod, she said, 'You find out what it is she loves about that particular dress, and see how you can adapt it to something that will work. And then you need tact by the bucketload.'

'Tactful.' He tipped his head on one side and looked at her. 'But you always say what you think.'

'I do. But you can do that in a nice way, without stomping on people.'

The corners of his mouth twitched. 'I'll remember that, the next time you don't mince your words with me.'

She laughed back. 'You're getting a bit more bearable, so I might be nicer to you.'

He bowed his head slightly. 'For the compliment.' Then he took her hand and lifted it to his mouth, pressed a kiss into her palm, and folded her fingers round it.

It made her knees go weak. To cover the fact that he flustered her, she asked, 'How was your day?'

'Full of meetings.'

No wonder he found it hard to relax and go with the flow. He was used to a ridiculously tight schedule.

But at least he seemed to relax more once they were in the capsule and rising to see a late summer evening view of London. Claire was happy just to enjoy the view, with Sean's arm wrapped round her.

'I was thinking,' he said softly. 'I owe you pudding and coffee. I have good coffee back at my place.'

'Would there be caramel hearts to go with it?' she asked hopefully.

'There might be,' he said, the teasing light back in his eyes.

This sounded like a spontaneous offer rather than being planned, she thought. So maybe it could make up for the earlier part of the evening. 'That sounds good,' she said. 'Coffee and good chocolate. Count me in.'

And, to her pleasure, he held her hand all the way back to his place. Now they weren't on a schedule any more, he was less driven—and she liked this side of him a lot more.

The last time Claire had been to Sean's house, she'd waited on the path outside while he picked up his luggage. This time, he invited her in. She discovered that his kitchen was very neat and tidy—as she'd expected—but it clearly wasn't a cook's kitchen. There were no herbs growing in pots, no ancient and well-used implements. She'd guess that the room wasn't used much beyond making drinks.

His living room was decorated in neutral tones. Claire was pleased to see that there were lots of family photographs on the mantelpiece, but she noticed that the art on the walls was all quite moody.

'It's Whistler,' he said, clearly realising what she was looking at. 'His nocturnes—I like them.'

'I would've pegged you as more of a Gainsborough man than a fan of tonalism,' she said.

He looked surprised. 'You know art movements?'

'I did History of Art for GCSE,' she said.

'Then again, I guess those paintings are a lot like you. They're understated and you really have to look to see what's there.'

'I'm not sure,' he said, 'if that was meant to be a compliment.'

'It certainly wasn't meant to be an insult,' she said. 'More a statement of fact.'

He poured them both a coffee, added sugar and a lot of milk to hers, and gestured to the little dish he'd brought on the tray. 'Caramel hearts, as you said you liked them.'

'I do.' She smiled at him, appreciating the fact that he'd remembered and made the effort.

'You can put on some music, if you like,' he suggested, indicating his MP3 player.

She skimmed through it quickly and frowned. 'Sean, I don't mean to be horrible, but all your playlists are a bit—well...'

'What?' he asked, sounding puzzled.

'They're named for different types of workouts, so I'm guessing all the tracks in each list have the same number of beats per minute.'

'Yes, but that's sensible. It means everything's arranged the way I want it for whatever exercise I'm doing.'

'I get that,' she said, 'but don't you enjoy music?'

He frowned. 'Of course I do.'

'I can't see what you listen to for pleasure.

To me this looks as if you only play set music at set times.' Regimented again. And this time she couldn't just let it go. 'That works for business but, Sean, you can't live your personal life as if it's a business.'

'Right,' he said tightly.

So much for reaching an understanding. She sighed. 'I'm not having a go at you. I'm just saying you're missing out on so much and maybe there's another way of doing things.'

'Let's agree to disagree, shall we?'

Sean had closed off on her again, Claire thought with an inward sigh—and now she could guess exactly why his girlfriends didn't last for much longer than three weeks. He'd drive them crazy by stonewalling them as soon as they tried to get close to him, and then either he'd gently suggest that they should be just friends, or they'd give up trying to be close to him.

She also knew that telling him that would be the quickest way of ending things between them; and from the few glimpses she'd had she was pretty sure that, behind his walls, the real Sean Farrell was someone really worth getting to know.

'OK, I'll back off,' she said. 'But you have absolutely nothing slushy and relaxing on here.'

He coughed. 'In case you hadn't noticed, I'm male.'

She'd noticed, all right.

'I don't do slushy,' he continued. 'But...' He took the MP3 player gently from her and flicked rapidly through the tracks.

When the music began playing, she recognised 'Can't Take My Eyes Off You', but it was a rock version of the song.

'The band played this at Ashleigh's wedding,' he said, 'and I found myself looking straight at you—that's why I asked you to dance.'

'And there was I thinking it was because it was traditional,' she deadpanned.

'No. I just wanted to dance with you.'

His honesty disarmed her. Just when he'd driven her crazy and she was thinking of calling the whole thing off, he did something like this that made her melt inside.

He drew her into his arms, and Claire was surprised to discover that, even though the song was fast, they could actually dance slowly to it.

'And then, when I was dancing with you,' he continued, 'I wanted to kiss you.'

She found herself moistening her lower lip with her tongue. 'Do you want to kiss me now, Sean?'

'Yes.' He held her gaze. 'And I want to do an awful lot more than just kiss you.'

Excitement thrummed through her, but she tried to play it cool. 'Could you be more specific?'

'I want to take that dress off,' he said, 'lovely as it is. And I want to kiss every inch of skin I uncover.'

'That sounds like a good plan,' she said. 'So what do I do?'

He smiled. 'I'm surprised you don't already know that one. Isn't it what you're always saying? Be spontaneous. Follow your heart. Go with the flow.'

'So that means,' she said, 'I get to take that prissy suit off you?'

'Prissy?' he queried. 'My suit's *prissy*?'

'It's beautifully cut, but it's so neat and tidy. I'd like to see you dishevelled,' she said, 'like you were that morning in Capri.'

'Would that be the morning you threw me out of your bed?'

'Yes, and don't make me feel guilty about it. That was mainly circumstances,' she said.

'Hmm.'

'Besides, I can't throw you out of your own bed,' she pointed out.

'Now that's impeccable logic.' He frowned.

'Though, actually, if you said no at any point I hope you realised I'd stop.'

She stroked his face. 'Sean, of course I know that. You're…'

'Dull?'

She shook her head. 'I was going to say honourable.'

He brushed the pad of his thumb across her lower lip, making her skin tingle. 'You normally call me regimented.'

'You can be. You were tonight, and I nearly left you to it and went home.' She smiled. 'But there's a huge difference between regimented and dull.'

'Is there?'

'Let me show you,' she said. 'Take me to bed.'

'I thought you'd never ask.'

To her surprise, he scooped her up and actually carried her up the stairs. She half wanted to make a snippy comment about him being muscle-bound, to tease him and push him, but at the same time she didn't want to spoil the moment. She was shocked to discover that she actually quite liked the way he was taking charge and being all troglodyte.

Once they were in his room, he set her down on her feet.

His bedroom was painted in shades of smoky

blue—very masculine, with a polished wooden floor, a rug in a darker shade that toned with the walls and matched the curtains, and limed oak furniture. But what really caught Claire's eye was his bed. A sleigh bed, also in limed oak, and she loved it. She'd always wanted a bed like that, but there really wasn't the room for that kind of furniture in her flat. Sean's Victorian terraced house was much more spacious and the bed was absolutely perfect.

'The last time you took your dress off for me,' he said, 'your underwear matched. Does it match today?'

'That's for me to know,' she said, 'and for you to find out.'

'Is that a challenge?'

'In part. It's also an offer.' She paused. 'Um, before this goes any further, do we have Monday's problem?'

'We absolutely do not,' he confirmed.

'Good.' Because she was going to implode if she had to wait much longer.

He drew the curtains and turned on the bedside light; it was a touch lamp, so he was able to dim the glow. Then he sat on the edge of the bed. 'Show me,' he invited.

She unzipped her dress and stepped out of it, then hung it over the back of a chair.

'What?' she asked, seeing the amusement in his face.

'You're a closet neat freak,' he said.

'No. Just practical. This is linen. It creases very, very badly. And I'm not walking out of here looking as if I've just been tumbled in a haystack.'

He gave her a slow, sexy smile. 'I like that image. Very much. You, tumbled in a haystack.'

She shook her head. 'It's not at all romantic, you know. Straw's prickly and itchy and totally unsexy.'

'And I assume you know that because you've, um, gone with the flow?'

'Listen, I haven't slept with everyone I've dated, and I certainly haven't slept with anyone else as fast as I fell into bed with *you*,' she said, folding her arms and giving him a level stare.

He stood up, walked over to her and brushed his mouth against hers. 'I'm not calling you a tart, Claire. We both have pasts. It's the twenty-first century, not the nineteen-fifties. I'm thirty and you're twenty-seven. I'd be more surprised if we were both still virgins.' He traced the lacy edge of her bra with one fingertip. 'Mmm. Cream lace. I like this. You have excellent taste in clothing, Ms Stewart.'

'It's oyster, not cream,' she corrected.

He grinned. 'And you have the cheek to call me prissy.'

'Details,' she said. 'You need to get them right.'

'We're in agreement there.'

She coughed.

'What?' he asked.

'I'm in my underwear. You can see that it matches, so I've done my half of the bargain. And right now, Mr Farrell, I have to say that you're very much overdressed.'

'So strip me, Claire,' he said, opening his arms to give her full access to his clothes.

It was an offer she wasn't going to refuse.

Afterwards, curled in Sean's arms, Claire turned her face so she could kiss his shoulder. 'I'd better go.'

'Not yet. This is comfortable.' He held her closer. 'Stay for a bit longer. I'll drive you home.'

So Sean the super-efficient businessman was a cuddler? Ah, bless, Claire thought. And, actually, she rather liked it. It made him that much more human. 'OK,' she said, and settled back against him.

Funny how they didn't really need to talk. Just being together was enough. It was *peace-*

ful. Something else she would never have believed about herself and Sean; but she liked just being with him. When he wasn't being super-organised down to the last microsecond. And it seemed that he felt the same.

So maybe, just maybe, this wasn't all going to end in tears.

When she finally got dressed and he drove her home, he parked outside her flat. 'So. When are you free next?' he asked.

'Sunday?' she suggested. 'I have the shop on Saturday.'

'Sunday works for me.'

'You organised tonight, so I'll organise Sunday,' she said. 'And that means doing things my way.'

'Going with the flow.' He looked slightly pained.

'It means being spontaneous and having fun,' she said. 'I'll pick you up at nine. And I won't be late.'

'No?' he asked wryly.

'No.' She kissed him. 'The first bit of tonight was, um, a bit much for me. But I loved dinner. I loved the London Eye and just being with you. Those kind of things works for me. It's just…' She shook her head. 'Schedules are for work. And I keep my work and my personal life separate.'

'Hmm,' he said, and she knew he wasn't convinced. But then he made the effort and said, 'I enjoyed being with you.'

But the fact she'd been late had really grated on him. He didn't have to tell her that.

He kissed her lightly. 'I'll walk you to your door.'

'Sean, it's half a dozen paces. I think I'm old enough to manage.'

He spread his hands. 'As you wish.'

'I'm not pushing you away,' she said softly. 'But I don't need protecting—the same as you don't.' She already had one overprotective male in her life, and that was more than enough for her. And it was half the reason why she'd always chosen free-spirited boyfriends who wouldn't make a fuss over everything or smother her.

Though maybe she'd gone too far the other way, because they'd all been disastrous.

But could Sean compromise? Could they find some kind of middle ground between them? If not, then this was going to be just as much a disaster as her previous relationships.

'Thank you for caring,' she said, knowing that his heart was in the right place—he just went a bit too far, that was all. 'I'll see you Sunday.'

'Spontaneous. Go with the flow.'

'You're learning. *Carpe diem*,' she said with a smile, and kissed him. 'Goodnight.'

CHAPTER NINE

WHEN CLAIRE WENT to pick Sean up on Sunday morning he was wearing formal trousers, a formal shirt and a tie. At least this time it wasn't a complete suit, but it still didn't work for what she wanted to do. And they looked totally mismatched, given that Claire was wearing denim shorts, a strappy vest and matching canvas shoes. Sean looked way too formal.

'Do you actually own a pair of jeans?' she asked.

'No.'

It was just as well she'd second-guessed. 'Right, then.' She delved into her tote bag and brought out a plastic carrier bag bearing the name of a department store.

'What's this?' he asked.

'Pressie. For you.' When he still looked blank, she added, 'The idea is that you wear it. As in right now.'

He looked in the bag. 'You bought me a pair of jeans?'

'Give the monkey a peanut,' she drawled.

'How do you know my size?'

She rolled her eyes. 'I measured you for a wedding suit, remember?'

He sighed. 'Claire, you didn't need to buy me a pair of jeans.'

'You don't own any. So actually, yes, I did.'

He looked at her, and she sighed. 'Sean, don't be difficult about this. I bought you a present, that's all. It's what people do when they date.'

He still didn't look convinced.

'Look, you bought me those gorgeous flowers, and I don't think you'd enjoy it if I bought you flowers—well, not that I think you *can't* buy a man flowers,' she clarified, 'but I don't think you're the kind of man who'd really appreciate them.'

'Probably not,' he admitted.

'Most people would buy their man some chocolate, but I can hardly give chocolate to someone who owns a confectionery company, can I? Which leaves me pretty stuck for buying you a gift. It's just an ordinary pair of jeans, Sean. Nothing ridiculously overpriced. So come on. Do something you haven't done since you were a teenager,' she coaxed, 'and wear the jeans. And swap those shoes for your running shoes.'

'My running shoes?' he queried.

She nodded. 'Because I bet you don't have a pair of scruffy, "go for a walk and it doesn't matter if they're not perfectly polished" shoes.'

'There's nothing wrong with looking smart at work,' he protested.

'I know, but you're not at work today, Sean. You're playing. You can keep the shirt, but lose the tie.'

'Bossy,' he grumbled, but he did as she asked. By the time he'd changed into the jeans and his running shoes, he looked fantastic—much more approachable. *Touchable.* Claire was glad she'd picked a light-coloured denim that looked slightly worn. It really, really suited him.

She folded her arms and looked at him.

'What now?' he asked. 'I'm not wearing the tie.'

'But your top button is still done up. Fix it, and roll your sleeves up.'

'Claire...'

'We did your date your way,' she said. 'And you agreed that we'd do this one my way.'

'This is the giddy limit,' he said, and for a moment she thought he was going to refuse; but finally he indulged her.

'That's almost perfect,' she said, then sashayed over to him, reached up to kiss him, and then messed up his hair.

'Why did you do that?' he asked, pulling back.

'It's the "just got out of bed" look. Which makes you look seriously hot,' she added. 'Like you did in Capri.'

He gave her a predatory smile. 'So if you think I look hot…'

'Rain check,' she said. 'Because we're going out and having fun, first.'

There was a bossy side to Claire, Sean thought, that he'd never seen before. The whole idea of giving up control—that just wasn't how he did things.

Claire Stewart was dangerous with a capital D where his peace of mind was concerned.

'This is your car?' He looked at the bright pink convertible Mini stencilled with daisies that was parked on the road outside his house. 'Oh, you are kidding me.'

'What's wrong with my car?' She put her finger into the keyring and spun her keys round.

What was wrong with the car? Where did he start?

He closed his eyes. 'OK. I know, I know,

go with the flow.' He groaned and opened his eyes again. 'But, Claire. *Pink*. With daisies. Really?'

Finally she took pity on him. 'I borrowed it from a friend. I don't have a car of my own at the moment.'

'Then we could go wherever it is in mine,' he suggested hopefully.

'Nope—we're doing this my way.' She gave him another of those insolent grins. 'Actually, my friend wants to sell this. I was thinking about buying it from her.'

He pulled a face, but said nothing.

'Very wise, Sean, very wise,' she teased.

She tied her hair back with a scarf, added some dark glasses that made her look incredibly sexy, and then added the disgusting khaki cap he remembered from Capri and which cancelled out the effect of the glasses. Once they were sitting in the car, she put the roof down, connected her MP3 player, and started blasting out sugary nineteen-sixties pop songs. Worse still, she made him sing along; and Sean was surprised to discover that he actually knew most of the songs.

By the time they got to Brighton, he'd stopped being embarrassed by the sheer loudness of the car and was word-perfect on the choruses of all her favourite songs.

'Brighton,' he said.

'Absolutely. Today is "Sean and Claire do the seaside",' she said brightly.

'And this isn't planned out?'

She rolled her eyes. 'Don't be daft—you don't plan things like going to the seaside. You go with the flow and you have *fun*.' She parked the car, then took his hand and they strolled across to the seafront.

This was so far removed from what he'd normally do on a Sunday. He might sit in his garden—perfectly manicured by the man he paid to mow the lawn, weed the flower beds, and generally make the area look tidy—but nine times out of ten he'd be in his study, working. He couldn't even remember the last time he went to the seaside. With one of his girlfriends, probably, but he hadn't paid much attention.

But with Claire, he was definitely paying attention.

He hung back slightly. 'Those are very *short* shorts.' And it made him want to touch her.

She just laughed. 'I have great legs—I might as well show them off before they go all wrinkly and saggy when I'm old.'

'You're…' He stopped and shook his head.

'I'm what, Sean?'

'A lot of things,' he said, 'half of which I wouldn't dare utter right now.'

'Chicken,' she teased.

'Discretion's the better part of valour,' he protested.

She laughed and took him onto the pier. They queued up to go on the fairground rides.

'You couldn't get fast-track tickets?' he asked.

She rolled her eyes. 'Queuing is part of the fun.'

'How?' he asked. In his view, queuing was a waste of time. If something was worth visiting, you bought fast-track tickets; otherwise, you didn't bother and you used your time more wisely.

'Anticipation,' she said. 'It'll be worth the wait.'

He wasn't so sure, but he'd agreed to do this her way. 'OK.'

But then they queued for the roller coaster.

'I thought you hated heights?'

'I do, but it'll be worth it if it loosens you up a little,' she said. 'It's OK to stop and smell the roses, Sean. If anything it'll enrich the time you spend on your business, because you'll look at things with a wider perspective.'

'Playing the business guru now, are you?'

'I don't play when it comes to business,'

she said, 'but I do remember to play in my free time.'

'Hmm.'

He wasn't that fussed about the thrill rides, but for her sake he pretended to enjoy himself.

They grabbed something quick to eat, then went over to the stony, steeply sloping beach next. The sea was such an intense shade of turquoise, they could have been standing on the shore of the Mediterranean rather than the English Channel. He'd never seen the sea in England look so blue. And this, he thought, was much more his style than waiting in a queue for a short thrill ride that did nothing to raise his pulse.

Claire, on the other hand, could seriously raise his pulse...

'Shoes off,' she said, removing her own canvas shoes, 'and roll up your jeans.'

'You're so bossy,' he grumbled.

She grinned. 'The reward will be worth it.'

'What reward?'

She fluttered her eyelashes at him. 'Wait and see.'

He had to admit that it was nice walking on the edge of the sea with her, his shoes in one hand and her hand in his other. The sound of the waves rushing onto the pebbles and the seagulls squawking, the scent of the sea air and the warmth of the sunlight on his skin. Right at that moment, he'd never felt more alive.

It must have shown in his face, because she said softly, 'Told you it was rewarding.'

'Uh-huh.' He smiled at her. 'Talking of rewards…' He leaned forward and kissed her. But what started out as a sweet, soft brush of her lips against his soon turned hot.

He pulled back, remembering that they were in a public place and with families around them. 'Claire. We need to…'

'I know.' Her fingers tightened round his. 'And this was what I wanted today. For you to let go, just a little bit, and have some fun with me.'

'I *am* having fun,' he said, half surprised by the admission.

'Good.' Her face had gone all soft and dreamy and it made him want to kiss her again—later, he promised himself.

When they'd finished paddling, they had to walk on the pebbles to dry off—Claire clearly hadn't thought to bring a towel with her—and then she said, 'Time for afternoon tea. And I have somewhere really special in mind.'

'OK.' He didn't mind going with the flow for a while, especially as it meant holding her hand. There was something to be said about just wandering along together.

As they walked into the town, he could see the exotic domes and spires of Brighton Pavilion.

Another queue, he thought with a sigh. It was one of the biggest tourist attractions in the area. Again, if she'd planned it they could've bought tickets online rather than having to queue up. He hated wasting time like this.

But, when they got closer, he realised there was something odd. No queues.

A notice outside the Pavilion informed them that the building was closed for urgent maintenance. Just for this weekend.

Sean just about stopped himself pointing out that if Claire had planned their trip in advance, then she would've known about this and she wouldn't have been disappointed.

'Oh, well,' she said brightly. 'I'm sure we can find a nice tea shop somewhere and have a traditional cream tea.'

Except all the tea shops nearby were full of tourists who'd had exactly the same idea. There were queues.

'Sorry. This is, um, a bit of a disaster,' she said.

Yes. But he wasn't going to make her feel any worse about it by agreeing with her.

'*Carpe diem,*' he said. 'Maybe there's an ice cream shop we can go to instead.'

'Maybe,' she said, though he could tell that she was really disappointed. He guessed that she'd wanted to share the gorgeous furnishings of the Pavilion with him—and there had probably been some kind of costume display, too.

They wandered through the historic part of the town, peeking in the windows of the antiques shops and little craft shops, and eventually found a tea shop that had room at one of the tables. Though as it was late afternoon, the tea shop had run out of scones and cream.

'Just the tea is fine, thanks,' Sean said with a smile.

They had a last walk along the beach, then Claire drove them home. 'Shall I drop you back at your house, or would you like to come back to my place and we can maybe order in some Chinese food?' she asked.

Given what she'd said to him by the sea, Sean knew what she wanted to hear. 'I think,' he said, 'we'll go with the flow.'

Her smile was a real reward—full of warmth and pleasure rather than smugness. 'We won't go home on the motorway, then,' she said. 'We'll find a nice little country pub where we can have dinner.'

Except it turned out that every pub they stopped at didn't do food on Sunday evenings.

'I can't believe this,' she said. 'I mean— it's the summer. Prime tourist season. Why on earth wouldn't any of them serve food on Sunday evenings?'

Sean didn't have the heart to ask why she hadn't planned it better. 'Go back on to the motorway,' he said. 'We'll get a takeaway back in London.'

'I'm so sorry. Still, at least we can keep the roof down and enjoy the sun on the way home,' Claire said.

Which was clearly all she needed to say to jinx it, because they were caught in a sudden downpour. By the time she'd found somewhere safe to stop and put the car's soft top back up, they were both drenched. 'I'm so sorry. That wasn't supposed to happen,' Claire said, biting her lip.

'So we were literally going with the flow. Of water,' Sean said, and kissed her.

'What was that for?' she asked.

'For admitting that you're not always right.' He stole another kiss. 'And also because that T-shirt looks amazing on you right now.'

'Because it's wet, you mean?' She rolled her eyes at him. 'Men.'

He smiled. 'Actually, I wanted to cheer you up a bit.'

'Because today's been a total disaster.'

'No, it hasn't. I enjoyed the sea.'

'But we didn't get to the Pavilion, we missed out on a cream tea, I couldn't find anywhere for dinner and we just got drenched.' She sighed. 'If I'd done things your way, it would've been different.'

'But when I planned our date, we ended up rushing and that was a disaster, too,' he said softly. 'I think we might both have learned something from this.'

'That sometimes you need to plan your personal life?' she asked.

'And sometimes you need to go with the flow,' he said. 'It's a matter of compromise.'

'That works for me, too. Compromise.' And her smile warmed him all the way through.

On the way back to London, he asked, 'So are you seriously going to buy this car?'

'What's wrong with it?'

'Apart from the colour? I was thinking, it's not very practical for transporting wedding dresses.'

'I don't need a car for that. I'm hiring a van for the wedding show,' she said.

'So why don't you have a car?' he asked.

'I live and work in London, so I don't really need one—public transport's fine.'

'You needed a car today to take us to the seaside,' he pointed out.

'Not necessarily. We could have gone by train,' she said.

'But then you wouldn't have been able to sing your head off all the way to Brighton.'

'And we wouldn't have got wet on the way home,' she agreed ruefully.

'We really need to get you out of those wet clothes,' he said, 'and my place is nearer than yours.'

'Good point,' she said, and drove back to his.

Sean had the great pleasure of peeling off her wet clothes outside the shower, then soaping her down under the hot water. When they'd finished, he put her clothes in the washer-dryer while she dried off. And then he had the even greater pleasure of sweeping her off her feet again, carrying her to his bed, and making love with her until they were both dizzy.

Afterwards, she was all warm and sweet in his arms. He stroked her hair back from her face. 'You were going to tell me how come you're not a doctor.'

'It just wasn't what I wanted to do,' she said.

'But you applied to study medicine at university.'

She shifted onto her side and propped herself on one elbow so she could look into his face. 'It was Dad's dream, not mine. It's a bit hard to resist pressure from your parents when you're sixteen. Especially when your father's a bit on the overprotective side.' She wrinkled her nose. 'Luckily I realised in time that you can't live someone else's dream for them. So I turned down the places I was offered and reapplied to design school.'

He frowned. 'But you were doing science A levels.'

'And Art,' she said. 'And the teacher who taught my textiles class at GCSE wrote me a special reference, explaining that even though I hadn't done the subject at A level I was more than capable of doing a degree. At my interview, I wore a dress I'd made and I also took a suit I'd made with me. I talked the interviewers through all the stitching and the cut and the material, so they knew I understood what I was doing. And they offered me an unconditional place.'

He could see the pain in her eyes, and drew her closer. 'So what made you realise you didn't want to be a doctor?'

'My mum.' Claire dragged in a breath. 'She

was only thirty-seven when she died, Sean.' Tears filmed her eyes. 'She barely made it past half the proverbial three score years and ten. In the last week of her life, when we were talking she held my hand and told me to follow my dream and do what my heart told me was the right thing.'

Which clearly hadn't been medicine.

Not knowing what to say, he just stroked her hair.

'Even when I was tiny, I used to draw dresses. Those paper dolls—mine were always the best dressed in class. I used to sketch all the time. I wanted to design dresses. Specifically, wedding dresses.'

He had a feeling he knew why she tended to fight with her father, now.

Her next words confirmed it. 'Dad said designers were ten a penny, whereas being a doctor meant I'd have a proper job for life.' She sighed. 'I know he had my best interests at heart. He had a tough upbringing, and he didn't want me ever to struggle with money, the way he did when he was young. But being a doctor was *his* dream, not mine. He said I could still do dressmaking and what have you on the side—but no way would I have had the time, not with the crazy hours that newly qualified doctors work. It was an all or nothing thing.' She grimaced. 'We had a huge fight over it. He said I'd just be wasting a degree if I studied textile design instead, and he gave me an ultimatum. Study medicine, and he'd support me through uni; study textiles, and he was kicking me out until I came to my senses.'

That sounded like the words of a scared man, Sean thought. One who wanted the best for his daughter and didn't know how to get that through to her. And he'd said totally the wrong thing to a teenage girl who'd just lost the person she loved most in the world and wasn't dealing with it very well. Probably because he was in exactly the same boat.

'That's quite an ultimatum,' Sean said, trying to find words that wouldn't make Claire think he was judging her.

'It was pretty bad at the time.' She paused. 'I talked to your mum about it.'

He was surprised. 'My mum?'

Claire nodded. 'She was lovely—she knew I was going off the rails a bit and I'd started drinking to blot out the pain of losing Mum, so she took me under her wing.'

Exactly what Sean would've expected from his mother. And now he knew why she'd been so insistent that he should look after Claire, the night of Ashleigh's eighteenth birthday party. She'd known the full story. And she'd known that she could trust Sean to do the right thing. To look after Claire when she needed it.

Claire smiled grimly. 'The drinking was also the worst thing I could have done in Dad's eyes, because his dad used to drink and gamble. I think that was half the reason why I did it, because I wanted to make him as angry as he made me. But your mum sat me down and told me that my mum would hate to see what I was doing to myself, and she made me see that the way I was behaving really wasn't helping the situation. I told her what Mum said about following my dream, and she asked me what I really wanted to do with my life. I showed her my sketchbooks and she said that my passion for needlework showed, and it'd be a shame to ignore my talents.' She smiled. 'And then she talked to Dad. He still didn't think that designing dresses was a stable career—he wanted me to have what he thought of as a "proper" job.'

'Does he still think that?' Sean asked.

'Oh, yes. And he tells me it, too, every so often,' Claire said, sounding both hurt and exasperated. 'When I left the fashion house where I worked after I graduated, he panicked that I wouldn't be able to make a go of my own business. Especially because there was a recession on. He wanted me to go back to uni instead.'

'And train to be a doctor?'

'Because then I'd definitely have a job for life.' She wrinkled her nose. 'But it's not just about the academic side of things. Sure, I could've done the degree and the post-grad training. But my heart wouldn't have been in it, and that wouldn't be fair to my patients.' She sighed. 'And I had a bit of a cash flow problem last year. I took a hit from a couple of clients whose cheques bounced. I still had to pay my suppliers for the materials and, um...' She wrinkled her nose. 'I could've asked Dad to lend me the money to tide me over, but then he would've given me this huge lecture about taking a bigger deposit from my brides and insisting on cash or a direct transfer to my account. Yet again he would've made me feel that he didn't believe in me and I'm not good enough to make it on my own. So I, um, sold my car. It kept me afloat.'

'And have you changed the way you take money?'

She nodded. 'I admit, I learned that one the hard way. Nowadays I ask for stage payments. But there's no real harm done. And Dad doesn't know about it so I avoided the lecture.' Again, Sean could see the flash of pain in her eyes. 'I just wish Dad believed in me a bit more. Gran and Aunty Lou believe in me. So does Ash.'

'So do I,' Sean said.

At her look of utter surprise, he said softly, 'Ashleigh's wedding dress convinced me. I admit, I had my doubts about you. Especially when you lost her dress. But you came up with a workable solution—and, when the original dress turned up, I could see just how talented you are. Mum was right about you, Claire. Yes, you could've been a perfectly competent doctor, but you would've ignored your talents—and that would've been a waste.'

Her eyes sparkled with tears. 'From you, that's one hell of a compliment. And not one I ever thought I'd hear. Thank you.'

'It's sincerely meant,' he said. 'You did the right thing, following your dreams.'

'I know I did. And I'm happy doing what I do. I'm never going to be rich, but I make enough for what I need—and that's important.' She paused. 'But what about you, Sean? What about your dreams?'

'I'm living them,' he said automatically.

'But supposing Farrell's didn't exist,' she persisted. 'What would you do then?'

'Start up another Farrell's, I guess,' he said.

'So toffee really is your dream?' She didn't sound as if she believed him.

'Of course toffee's my dream. What's wrong with that?' he asked.

'You're the fourth generation to run the business, Sean,' she said softly. 'You have a huge sense of family and heritage and integrity and duty. Even if you didn't really want to do it, you wouldn't walk away from your family business. Ever.'

It shocked him that she could read him so accurately. Nobody else ever had. She wasn't judging him; she was just stating facts. 'I like my job,' he protested. He *did*.

'I'm not saying you don't,' she said softly. 'I'm just asking you, what's your dream?'

'I'm living it,' he said again. Though now she'd made him question that.

It was true that he would never have walked away from the business, even if his parents hadn't been killed. He'd always wanted to be part of Farrell's. It was his heritage.

But, if he was really honest about it, he'd felt such pressure to keep the business going the same way that his father had always run things. After his parents had died in the crash, he'd needed to keep things stable for everyone who worked in the business, and keeping to the way things had always been done seemed the best way to keep everything on a stable footing.

He'd been so busy keeping the business going. And then, once he'd proved to his staff and his competitors that he was more than capable of running the business well, he'd been so busy making sure that things stayed that way that he just simply hadn't had the time to think about what he wanted.

Just before his parents' accident, he'd been working on some new product ideas. Something that would've been his contribution to the way the family business developed. He'd loved doing the research and development work. But he'd had to shelve it all after the accident, and he'd never had time to go back to his ideas.

Though it was pointless dwelling on might-have-beens. Things were as they were. And the sudden feeling of uncertainty made him antsy.

Sean had intended to ask Claire to stay, that night; but right at that moment he needed some distance between them, to get his equilibrium back. 'I'd better check to see if your clothes are dry.'

They were. So it was easy to suggest making a cold drink while she got dressed. Easier still to hint that it was time for her to go home—particularly as Claire took the hint.

He let her walk out of the door without kissing her goodbye.

And he spent the rest of the evening wide awake, miserable and regretting it. She'd pushed him and he'd done what he always did and closed off, not wanting her to get too close.

But her words went round and round in his head. *What's your dream?*

The problem was, you couldn't always follow your dreams. Not if you had responsibilities and other people depended on you.

Everybody has a dream, Sean.

What did he really want?

He sat at his desk, staring out of the window at a garden it was too dark to see. Then he gritted his teeth, turned back to his computer and opened a file.

Dreams were a luxury. And he had a business to run—one that had just managed to survive a takeover bid. Dreams would have to wait.

CHAPTER TEN

SEAN SPENT THE next day totally unable to concentrate.

Which was ridiculous because he never, but never, let any of his girlfriends distract him from work.

But Claire Stewart was different, and she got under his skin in a way that nobody ever had before. He definitely wasn't letting her do it, but it was happening all the same—and he really didn't know what to do about it.

Part of him wanted to call her because he wanted to see her; and part of him was running scared because she made him look at things in his life that he'd rather ignore.

And he still couldn't get her words out of his head. *Everybody has a dream, Sean.* Just what was his?

He still hadn't worked out what to say to her by the evening, so he buried himself in work instead. And he noticed that she hadn't called him, either. So did that mean she, too, thought this was turning out to be a seriously bad idea and they ought to end it?

And then, on Tuesday morning, his PA brought him a plain white box.

'What's this?' he asked.

Jen shrugged. 'I have no idea. I was just asked to give it to you.'

There was no note with the box. He frowned. 'Who brought it?'

'A blonde woman. She wouldn't give her name. She said you'd know who it was from,' Jen said.

His heart skipped a beat.

Claire.

But if Claire had actually come to the factory and dropped this off personally, why hadn't she come to see him?

Or maybe she thought he'd refuse to see her. They hadn't exactly had a fight on Sunday evening, but he had to acknowledge that things had been a little bit strained when she'd left. Maybe this was her idea of a parley, the beginning of some kind of truce.

And hadn't she said about not sending him flowers and how you couldn't give chocolates to a confectioner?

'Thank you. I have a pretty good idea who

it's from,' he said to Jen, and waited until she'd closed the door behind her before opening the box.

Claire had brought him cake.

Not just cake—the most delectable lemon cake he'd ever eaten in his life.

He gave in and called her business line.

She answered within three rings. 'Dream of a Dress, Claire speaking.'

'Thank you for the cake,' he said.

'Pleasure.'

Her voice was completely neutral, so he couldn't tell her mood. Well, he'd do things her way for once and ask her straight out. 'Why didn't you come in and say hello?'

'Your PA said you were in a meeting, and I didn't really have time to wait until you were done.'

'Fair enough.' He paused. He knew what he needed to say, and he was enough of a man not to shirk it. 'Claire, I owe you an apology.'

'What for?'

'Pushing you away on Sunday night.'

'Uh-huh.'

He sighed, guessing what she wanted him to say. 'I still can't answer your question.'

'Can't or won't?'

'A bit of both, if I'm honest,' he said.

'OK. Are you busy tonight?'

'Why?' he asked.

'I thought we could go and smell some roses.'

Claire-speak for having some fun, he guessed.

'Can you meet me at my place?'

'Sure. Would seven work for you?'

'Fine. Don't eat,' she said, 'because we can probably grab something on the way. Some of the food stalls at Camden Lock will still be open at that time.'

Clearly she intended to take him for a walk somewhere. 'And is this a jeans and running shoes thing?' he checked.

'You can wear your prissiest suit and your smartest shoes—whatever you like, as long as you can walk for half an hour or so and still be comfortable.'

When Sean turned up at her shop at exactly seven o'clock, Claire was wearing a navy summer dress patterned with daisies and flat court shoes. Her hair was tied back with another chiffon scarf—clearly that was Claire's favoured style—but he was pleased that she didn't add her awful khaki cap, this time. Instead, she just donned a pair of dark glasses.

They walked down to Camden Lock, grabbed

a burger and shared some polenta fries, then headed along the canalside towards Regent's Park. He'd never really explored the area before, and it was a surprisingly pretty walk; some of the houses were truly gorgeous, and all the while there were birds singing in the trees and the calm presence of the canal.

'I love the walk along here. It's only ten minutes or so between the lock and the park,' she said.

And then Sean discovered that Claire had meant it literally about coming to smell the roses when she took him across Regent's Park to Queen Mary's Garden.

'This place is amazing—it's the biggest collection of roses in London,' she told him.

There were pretty bowers, huge beds filled with all different types of roses, and walking through them was like breathing pure scent; it totally filled his senses.

'This is incredible,' he said. 'I didn't think you meant it literally about smelling the roses.'

'I meant it metaphorically as well—you must know that WH Davies poem, "What is this life if full of care, We have no time to stand and stare,",' she said. 'You have to make time for things like this, Sean, or you miss out on so much.'

He knew she had a point. 'Yeah,' he said softly, and tightened his fingers round hers.

He could just about remember coming to see the roses in Regent's Park as a child, but everything since his parents' death was a blur of work, work and more work.

Six years of blurriness.

Being with Claire had brought everything into sharp focus again. Though Sean wasn't entirely sure he liked what he saw when he looked at his life—and it made him antsy. Claire was definitely dangerous to his peace of mind.

She drew him over to look at the borders of delphiniums, every shade of white and cream and blue through to almost black.

'Now these I *really* love,' she said. 'The colour, the shape, the texture—everything.'

He looked at her. 'So you're a secret gardener?'

'Except doing it properly would take time I don't really have to spare,' she said. 'Though, yes, if had a decent-sized garden I'd plant it as a cottage garden with loads of these and hollyhocks and foxgloves, and tiny little lily-of-the-valley and violets.'

'These ones here are exactly the same colour as your eyes.'

She grinned. 'Careful, Sean. You're waxing a bit poetic.'

Just to make the point, he kissed her.

'Tsk,' she teased. 'Is that the only way you have to shut me up?'

'It worked for Benedick,' he said.

'*Much Ado* is a rom-com—and I thought you said you didn't like rom-coms?'

'I said I didn't mind ones with great dialogue—and dialogue doesn't get any better than Beatrice.' He could see Claire playing Beatrice; he'd noticed that she often had that deliciously acerbic bite to her words.

'And it's a good plot,' she said, 'except Hero ends up with a man who isn't good enough for her. I hate the bit where Claudio shames her on their wedding day, and it always makes me want to yell to her, "Don't do it!" at the end when she marries him.'

'They were different times and different mores, though I do know what you mean,' he said. 'I wouldn't want Ashleigh to marry a weak, selfish man.'

She winced. 'Like Rob Riverton. And I introduced her to him.'

'Not one of your better calls,' Sean said.

'I know.' She looked guilty. 'I did tell her to dump him because he wasn't good enough for her and he didn't treat her properly.'

A month ago, Sean wouldn't have believed that. Now, he did, because he'd seen for himself that Claire had integrity. 'Claire,' he said, yanked her into his arms and kissed her.

'Was that to shut me up again?' she asked when he broke the kiss.

'No—it was because you're irresistible.'

She clearly didn't know what to say to that, because it silenced her.

They walked back along the canalside to Camden, hand in hand; then he bought them both a glass of wine and they sat outside, enjoying the late evening sunshine before walking back to her flat.

'Do you want to come in?' she asked.

'Is that wise?'

'Probably not, but I'm asking anyway.'

'Probably not,' he agreed, 'but I'm saying yes.'

They sat with the windows open, the curtains open and music playing; there was a jug of iced water on the coffee table, and she'd put frozen slices of lime in the jug. Sean was surprised by how at home he felt here; the room was decorated in very girly colours, compared to his own neutral colour scheme, but he felt as if he belonged.

'It's getting late. I ought to go,' he said softly. 'I have meetings, first thing.'

'You don't have to go,' Claire said. 'You could stay.' She paused. 'If you want to.'

'Are you sure?'

'I'm sure.'

In answer, he closed her curtains and carried her to her bed.

The next morning, Claire woke before her alarm went off to find herself alone in bed, and Sean's side of the bed was stone cold. She was a bit disappointed that he hadn't even woken her before he left, or put a note on the pillow. Then again, he'd said that he had early meetings. He'd probably left at some unearthly hour and hadn't wanted to disturb her sleep.

At that precise moment he walked in, carrying a tray with two paper cups of coffee and a plate of pastries. 'Breakfast is served, my lady.'

'You went out to buy us breakfast? That's— that's so *lovely*,' she said, sitting up, 'but you really didn't have to. I have fruit and yoghurt in the fridge, plus bread and granola in the cupboard.'

'I noticed a bakery round the corner from yours. I thought croissants might be nice, and I'm running a bit short on time so I bought the coffee rather than making it.'

'That sounds to me like an excuse for having decadent tendencies,' she teased.

He laughed back. 'Maybe.'

He sat on the bed and shared the almond-filled croissants with her. 'You thought I'd gone without saying goodbye, didn't you?'

'Um—well, yes,' she admitted.

'I wouldn't do that to you. I would at least have left you a note.' He finished his coffee and kissed her lightly. 'Sorry. I really *do* have to go now. Can I call you later?'

'I'd like that.' Claire wrapped herself in her robe so she could pad barefoot to the kitchen with him and kiss him goodbye at her front door.

She still couldn't quite get over the fact he'd gone out to buy them a decadent breakfast. And he'd stayed last night. This thing between them was moving so incredibly fast; it scared and exhilarated her at the same time. She guessed it would be the same for Sean. But would it scare him enough to make him push her away again, the way he had the other night? Or would he finally let her in?

They were both busy during the week, but Sean texted her on Friday.

Do you have any appointments over lunch?

Sorry, yes.

And, regretfully, she wasn't playing hard to get. She really did have appointments that she couldn't move.

OK. Are you busy after work?

Yes, but that was something she could move.

Why?

Am trying to be like you and plan a spontaneous date.

She couldn't help laughing. Planning and spontaneity didn't go together.

OK.

Cinema? he suggested.

Depends. Is popcorn on offer?

Could be... he texted back.

Deal. Time and place?

Can pick you up.

She wanted to keep at least some of her independence.

Saves time if I meet you there.

OK. Will check out films and text you where and when.

Claire had expected him to choose some kind of noir movie, but when she got to the cinema and met him with a kiss she discovered that he'd picked a rom-com.

'Is this to indulge me?' she asked.

'I've seen this one before. The structure's good and the acting's good,' he said.

'You're such a film snob,' she teased, but it warmed her that he'd thought of what she'd enjoy rather than imposing his choices on her regardless.

They sat in the back row, holding hands, and Claire enjoyed the film thoroughly. Back at his place afterwards, they were curled in bed together, when Sean said, 'I had a focus group meeting today.'

She remembered the samples he'd given her. 'Did it go how you wanted?'

'Not really,' he said. 'We need a rethink.'

'For what it's worth, I've always thought that your caramel hearts would be great as bridal favours. That's the sort of thing my brides always ask me if I know about, because not everyone likes the traditional sugared almonds.'

'Bridal favours?' he queried.

'Uh-huh—the hearts could be wrapped in silver or gold foil, and you can offer a choice of organza bags with them in say white, silver or gold, so brides can buy the whole package. They could be ordered direct from your website, or you could offer the special bridal package through selected shops.'

He nodded. 'That's brilliant, Claire. Thank you. I never even considered that sort of thing.'

'Why would you, unless you were connected to a wedding business?' she pointed out.

'I guess not.'

'So why didn't the focus group like the salted caramels? I thought they were fabulous.'

'It's a move too far from the core business. Farrell's has produced hard toffee for generations. We're not really associated with chocolates, apart from the caramel hearts—which were my mum's idea.'

'Are you looking to move away from making toffee, then?'

'Yes and no,' he said. 'What I want to do is look at other sorts of toffee.'

She frowned. 'Am I being dense? Because toffee's—well—toffee.'

'Unless it's in something,' he said. 'Toffee popcorn, like the one you chose tonight at the cinema. Or toffee ice cream.'

'You weren't concentrating on the film, were you?' she asked. 'You were thinking about work.'

'I was thinking about you, actually,' he said. 'But the toffee popcorn did set off a light-bulb in the back of my head.' He wrinkled his nose. 'If I took the business in that direction, it'd mean buying a whole different set of machinery and arranging a whole different set of staff training. I'd need to be sure that the investment would be worth the cost and Farrell's would see a good return on the money.'

'Unless,' she said, 'you collaborated with other manufacturers—ones who already have the factory set-up and the staff. Maybe you could license them to use your toffee.'

'That's a great idea. And I could draw up a shortlist of other family-run businesses whose ideas and ethos are the same as Farrell's. People who'd make good business partners.'

'That's your dream, isn't it?' she asked

softly. 'To keep your heritage—but to put your own stamp on it.'

'I guess. Research and development was always my favourite thing,' he admitted. 'I wanted to look at developing different flavours of toffee. Something different from mint, treacle, orange or nut. I was thinking cinnamon or ginger for Christmas, or maybe special seasonal editions of the chocolate hearts—say a strawberries and cream version for summer.'

'That's a great idea,' she said. 'Maybe white chocolate.'

'And different packaging,' he said. 'Something to position Farrell's hearts as the kind of thing you buy as special treats.'

'You could sell them in little boxes as well as big ones,' she said. 'For people who want a treat but don't want a big box.'

He kissed her. 'I'm beginning to think that I should employ you on my R and D team.'

'Now that,' she said, 'really wouldn't work. I'm used to doing things my way and I'd hate to have to go by someone else's rules all the while. Besides, I don't want you bossing me about and I think we'd end up fighting.'

He wrinkled his nose. 'I don't want to fight with you, Claire—I like how things are now.'

'Me, too,' she admitted.

'Make love, not war—that's a great slogan, you know.'

She grinned. 'Just as long as it's not all talk and no action, Mr Farrell.'

He laughed. 'I can take a hint.' And he kissed her until she was dizzy.

CHAPTER ELEVEN

OVER THE NEXT couple of weeks, Claire and Sean grew closer. Claire didn't get to see Sean every evening, but she talked to him every day and found herself really looking forward to the times they did see each other. And even on days when things were frustrating and refused to go right, or she had a client who changed her mind about what she wanted at least twice a day, it wasn't so bad because Claire knew she would be seeing Sean or talking to him later.

And he indulged her by taking her to one of her favourite places—the Victoria and Albert Museum. She took him to see her favourite pieces of clothing, showing him the fabrics, the shapes and the stitching that had inspired some of her own designs. When they stopped for a cold drink in the café, she looked at him.

'Sorry. I rather went into nerd mode. You should have told me to shut up.'

He smiled. 'Actually, I really enjoyed it.'

'But I was lecturing you, making you look at fiddly bits and pieces that probably bored you stupid.'

'You were lit up, Claire. Clothing design is your passion. And it was a privilege to see it,' he said softly. He reached across the table, took her hand and drew it to his lips. 'Don't ever lose that passion.'

He'd accepted her for who she was, Claire thought with sudden shock. The first man she'd ever dated who'd seen who she was, accepted it, and encouraged her to do what she loved.

In turn, Sean gave her a personal guided tour of the toffee factory. 'I'm afraid the white coat and the hair covering are non-negotiable,' he said.

'Health and safety. This is a working factory. And the clothes are about function, not form—just as they should be,' she said.

'I guess.' He took her through the factory, explaining what the various stages were and letting her taste the different products.

'I love the fact you're still using your great-grandparents' recipe for the toffee,' she said. 'And the photographs.' She'd noticed the blown-up photographs from years before lining the walls in the reception area. 'It's lovely to see that connection over the years.'

'A bit like you,' he said, 'and the way you hand-decorate a dress exactly the same as they would've done it two hundred years ago.'

'I guess.'

They were halfway through when Sean's sales manager came over.

'Sean, I'm really sorry to interrupt,' he said, smiling acknowledgement at Claire. 'I'm afraid we've got a bit of a situation.'

'Hey—don't mind me,' Claire said. 'The business comes first. I can do a tour at any time.'

'Thanks,' Sean said. 'What's the problem, Will?'

'I had the press on the phone earlier, talking about the takeover bid,' Will said. 'I explained that it's not happening and Farrell's is carrying on exactly as before, but someone's clearly been spreading doubts among our biggest customers, because I've been fielding phone calls ever since. And one of our customers in particular says he wants to talk to the organ grinder, not the monkey.'

'You're my sales manager,' Sean said. 'Which makes you as much of an organ grinder as I am.'

Will looked awkward. 'Not in Mel Archer's eyes.'

'Ah. *Him.*' Sean grimaced. 'Claire, would you mind if I let Will finish the tour with you?'

'Sure,' she said.

'I'll talk to Archer and explain the situation to him,' Sean said. 'And I'll make it very clear to him that I trust my senior team to do their jobs well and use their initiative.'

'Sorry.'

'It's not your fault,' Sean said. 'I'll see you later, Claire.'

She smiled at him. 'No worries. I'll wait for you in reception.'

'Sorry. It's the monkey rather than the organ grinder for you, too,' Will said.

She smiled. 'Sean says you're an organ grinder. That's good enough for me.'

Will finished taking her round and answered all her questions. Including ones she knew she probably shouldn't ask but couldn't help herself; this was a chance to see another side of Sean.

'So have you worked for Sean for long?' she asked Will.

'Three years,' Will said. 'And he's probably the best manager I've ever worked with. He doesn't micromanage—he trusts you to get on and do your job, though he's always there if things get sticky.'

'Which I guess they would be, in a toffee factory,' Claire said with a smile.

Will laughed. 'Yeah. Pun not actually intended. What I mean is he knows the business inside out. He's there if you need support, and if there's a problem you can't solve he'll have an answer—though what he does is ask you questions to make you think a bit more about it and work it out for yourself.'

So her super-efficient businessman liked to teach people and develop his staff, too. And it was something she knew he wouldn't have told her himself.

From the half of the tour Sean had given her and the insights Will added, Claire realised that maybe Sean really was living his dream; he really did love the factory and his job, and not just because it was his heritage and he felt duty-bound to preserve it for the next generation. Though she rather thought that if he'd had a choice in the matter, he would've worked in the research and development side of the business.

'He's a good man,' she said, meaning it.

When Ashleigh and Luke returned from their honeymoon, they invited Claire over to see the wedding photographs. She arrived bearing champagne and brownies. Sean was there already, and she gave him a cool nod of acknowledgement before cooing over the photographs and choosing the ones she wanted copies of.

A little later, he offered to help her make coffee. 'Have I done something to upset you?' he asked softly when they were alone in Ashleigh's kitchen.

'No.' Clare frowned. 'What makes you think that?'

'Just you seemed a little cool with me tonight.'

'In front of Ash, yes—she expects me to be just on the verge of civil with you. If I'm nice to you, she's going to guess something's going on, and I don't want her to know about this.' Claire took a deep breath. 'She's already asked me a couple of questions, and I told her we came to a kind of truce in Capri—once you realised it wasn't my fault her wedding dress disappeared—and you were one step away from grovelling.'

'You told her I was *grovelling*?'

Claire grinned. 'She just laughed and said grovelling isn't in your vocabulary, and she'd give it a week before we started sniping at each other again.'

He moved closer. 'I'm definitely not grovelling, but I'm not sniping either.' He paused. 'In fact, I'd rather just kiss you.'

'I'd rather that, too,' she said softly, 'but I'm not ready for Ash to know about this yet.'

'So I'm your dirty little secret?'

'For now—and I'm yours,' she said.

At the end of the evening, Sean said, 'Claire, it's raining—I'll give you a lift home to save you getting drenched.'

'This is quite some truce,' Ashleigh said, giving them both a piercing look. 'Though you probably won't make it back to Claire's before the ceasefire ends.'

'I won't fight if she doesn't,' Sean said. 'Claire?'

'No fighting, and thank you very much for the offer of the lift.'

Ashleigh narrowed her eyes at both of them, but didn't say any more.

'Do you have any idea how close you were to breaking our cover?' Claire asked crossly on the way home. 'I'm sure Ash has guessed.'

'What's your problem with anyone knowing about you and me?' Sean asked.

'Because it's still early days. And, actually, unless my calendar's wrong, you'll be dumping me in the next few days anyway.'

'How do you work that out?'

'Because, Sean Farrell, you never date anyone for more than three weeks in a row.'

'I don't dump my girlfriends exactly three weeks in to a relationship,' he said. 'That's a little old and a little unfair.'

'But you dump them,' Claire persisted.

'No, I break up with them nicely and I make them feel it's their decision,' he corrected.

'When it's actually yours.'

He shrugged. 'If it makes them feel better about the situation, what's the problem?'

'You're impossible.'

He laughed. 'Ashleigh said we wouldn't make it back to your place before we started fighting. She was right.'

'I'm not fighting, I'm just making a statement of facts—and don't you dare kiss me to shut me up,' she warned.

'I can't kiss you when I'm driving,' Sean pointed out, 'so that's a rain check.'

'You really are the most exasperating…' Unable to think of a suitable retort, she lapsed into silence.

'Besides,' he said softly, 'you'd be bored to tears with a yes-man or a lapdog.'

'Lapdog?' she asked, not following.

'"When husbands or when lapdogs breathe their last." Alexander Pope,' he explained helpfully.

She rolled her eyes. 'I forgot you did English A level.'

'And dated a couple of English teachers.'

'Would one of those have been the one who made you see a certain rom-com more than once?'

'Yes. At least you haven't done that.'

'You're still impossible,' she grumbled.

'Yup,' he said cheerfully.

'And, excuse me, you just missed the turning to my place.'

'Because we're not going to your place. We're going to mine.'

'But I have a bride coming in first thing tomorrow morning for a final fitting,' she protested.

'I have a washer-dryer, an alarm clock, a spare unused toothbrush, and I'll run you home after breakfast.'

She sighed. 'You've got an answer for everything.'

'Most things,' he corrected, and she groaned.

'I give up.'

'Good,' he said.

He stripped her very slowly once he'd locked his front door behind them, put her clothes in the laundry, then took her to bed. And he was as good as his word, finding her a spare toothbrush, making her coffee in the morning, making sure her clothes were dried, and taking her home.

She kissed him lingeringly in the car. 'See you later. And thanks for the lift.'

Ashleigh dropped by at lunchtime.

'Well, hello, stranger—long time, no see,' Claire teased. 'What is it, a little over twelve hours?'

'We're having lunch,' Ashleigh said. 'Now.'

'Why does this feel as if you're about to tell me off?' Claire asked.

'Because I am. When did this all happen?'

Claire tried to look innocent. 'When did all what happen?'

'You know perfectly well what I mean. You and my brother. And don't deny it. You're both acting totally out of character round each other.'

'He just gave me a lift home last night,' Claire said, crossing her fingers under the table. It had been a lot more than that.

'Hmm.' Ashleigh folded her arms and gave Claire a level stare.

Claire gave in. 'Ash, it's early days. And you know Sean; it's probably not going to last.'

'Why didn't you tell me?'

'Because when it all goes wrong I don't want our friendship to be collateral damage.'

Ashleigh hugged her. 'Idiot. Nothing would stop me being friends with you.'

'Sean doesn't want you to be collateral damage, either,' Claire pointed out.

Ashleigh rolled her eyes. 'I won't be, and don't you go overprotective on me like my big brother is—remember I'm older than you.'

'OK,' Claire said meekly.

'I thought something was up when he helped you make coffee, and then when he offered you a lift home…I knew it for sure,' Ashleigh said.

'It's still really, really early days,' Claire warned.

'But it's working,'

'At the moment. We still fight, but it's different now.' Claire smiled. 'Sean's not quite as regimented as I thought he was.'

Ashleigh laughed. 'Not with you around, he won't be.'

'And he's stopped calling me the Mistress of Chaos.'

'Good, because you're not.' Ashleigh hugged her again. 'I can't think of anyone I'd like more as my sister-in-law. I've always thought of you as like my sister anyway.'

'We haven't been together long,' Claire warned, 'so I'm not promising anything.'

'I think,' Ashleigh said, 'that you'll be good for each other.'

'Promise me you won't say anything? Even to Luke?'

'It's a bit too late for Luke,' Ashleigh said, 'but I won't say anything to Sean.'

'Thank you. And you'll be the first to know if things move forward. Or,' Claire said, 'when we break up.'

In the two weeks before the wedding show Claire was crazily busy and had almost no free time for dates. Sean took over and brought in takeaways to make sure she ate in the evenings; he also made her take breaks before her eyes started hurting, and gave her massages when her shoulders ached.

Even though part of Claire thought he was being just a little bit overprotective, she was grateful for the TLC. 'I really appreciate this, Sean.'

'I know, and you'd do the same for me if I had an exhibition,' he pointed out. 'By the way, I'm in talks with a couple of manufacturers about joint projects and licensing. Talking to you and brainstorming stuff like that,' he said, 'really helped me see the way I want the company to go in the future.'

'Following your dreams?'

'Maybe,' he said with a smile, and kissed her.

The week before the wedding show, Claire took Sean to meet her family—her father, her grandmother, Aunt Lou and her cousins. Clearly she'd talked to them about him, Sean thought, because they already seemed to know who he was and lots about him. Then he realised that they knew Ashleigh and his background was the same as hers.

Even though they were warm and welcoming and treated him as if he were one of them, chatting and laughing and teasing him, he still felt strange. His grandparents would've been older than Claire's and had died when he was in his teens. This was the first time for years that Sean had been in a family situation where he wasn't being the protective big brother and the head of the family, and it made him feel lost, not knowing quite where he was supposed to fit in.

It didn't help that Claire's father grilled him mercilessly about his intentions towards Claire. Sean could understand it—he shared Jacob's opinion of Claire's previous boyfriends, at least the ones that he'd met—but it still grated that he'd be judged alongside them.

And he could also see what Claire meant about her dad not believing in her. Jacob didn't see the point of spending time and money making six sets of wedding clothes that hadn't actually been ordered by clients, and he'd said a couple of times during the evening that he couldn't see how Claire would possibly get a return on her investment. Claire had smiled sweetly and glossed over it, but Sean had seen that little pleat between her brows that only appeared when she was really unhappy about something. Clearly she was hurt by the way her father still didn't believe in her.

Well, maybe he could give Jacob Stewart something to think about. 'I always do trade shows,' he said. 'They're really good for awareness—and it makes new customers consider stocking you when they see the quality of your product.'

'Maybe,' Jacob said.

'I don't know if you saw the dress Claire made for my sister, but it was absolutely amazing. She's really good at what she does. And what gives her the extra edge is that she loves what she does, too. That gives her clients confidence. And it's why they tell all their friends about her. Her referral rate is stunning.'

Jacob said nothing, but raised an eyebrow.

Sean decided not to push it any further—the last thing he wanted was for Jacob to upset Claire any further on the subject and knock her confidence at this late stage—but he had to hide a smile when he saw the fervent thumbs-up that Claire's grandmother and aunt did out of Jacob's viewpoint.

Though he was quiet when he drove Claire home.

'I'm sorry, Sean. I shouldn't have asked you to meet them—it's too early,' she said, guessing why he was quiet and getting it totally wrong. 'It's just, well, they'll all be coming to the wedding show and I thought it'd be better if you met them before rather than spring it on you then.'

'No, it was nice to meet them,' he said. 'I liked them.' He wanted to shake her father, but judged it not the most tactful thing to say.

'They liked you—and Dad approved of you, which has to be a first.'

He couldn't hide his surprise. 'Even though I argued with him?'

'You batted my corner,' she said. 'And I appreciate that. I think he did, too. Dad's just… a bit difficult.'

'He'll come round in the end,' Sean said.

'When he sees your collection on the catwalk, he'll understand.'

'Hardly. He's a guy. So he's not the slightest bit interested in dresses,' Claire said, though to Sean's relief this time she was smiling rather than looking upset. 'I just have to remember not to let it get to me.'

'You're going to be brilliant,' Sean said. 'Come on. Let's go to bed.'

She smiled. 'I thought you'd never ask...'

Over the next week, Claire worked later and later on last-minute changes to the wedding show outfits, and the only way Sean could get her out of her workroom for dinner was to haul her manually over his shoulder and carry her out of the room.

'You need to eat to keep your strength up, and you can't live off sandwiches for the next week,' he told her, 'or you'll make yourself ill.'

'I guess.' She blinked as she took in the fact that her kitchen was actually being used and something smelled gorgeous. 'Hang on, dinner isn't a takeaway.'

'It's nothing fancy, either,' Sean said dryly, 'but it's home-cooked from scratch and there are proper vegetables.' He gave her a rueful smile. 'And at least you have gadgets that help.'

'My electric steamer. Best gadget ever.' She smiled back and stroked his face. 'Sean, thank you. It's really good of you to do this for me.'

'Any time, and you know you'd do the same if I was the one up to my eyes in preparation for a big event, so it's not a big deal.' He kissed her lightly. 'Sit down, milady, because dinner will be served in about thirty seconds.'

But when he'd dished up and they were eating, he noticed that she was pushing her food around her plate. 'Is my cooking that terrible? You don't have to be polite with me—leave it if you hate it.'

'It's wonderful. I'm just tired.' She made an effort to eat.

He tried to distract her a little. 'So do you have a dream of a dress?'

'Not really,' she said.

'So all these years when you've sketched wedding dresses, you never once drew the one you wanted for yourself?'

'I guess it would depend when and where I got married—if it was on a beach in the Seychelles I wouldn't pick the same dress, veil or shoes as I'd pick for a tiny country church in the middle of winter in, say, the far north of Scotland.'

'I guess,' he said. 'So which kind of wedding would you prefer?'

'It's all academic,' she said.

He could guess why she wasn't answering him—she was obviously worried he'd think she was hinting and had expectations where he was concerned.

'Is that why the outfits in your wedding collection are so diverse?'

'Yes—four seasonal weddings, one vintage-inspired outfit, and one that's more tailored towards a civil wedding,' she explained.

'That's a good range,' he said. 'It will show people what you can do.'

'I hope so.' For a second she looked really worried and vulnerable.

'Claire, you know your stuff, you're good at what you do and your work is really going to shine at the show.' He reached over to squeeze her hand. 'I believe in you.'

'Thank you, though I wasn't fishing for compliments.'

'I know you weren't, and I was being sincere.'

'Sorry.' She wrinkled her nose. 'Ignore me. It's just a bit of stage fright, or whatever the catwalk equivalent is.'

'Which is totally understandable, given that it's your first show.' He cleared their plates away. 'Let me get you some coffee.'

She gave him a tired smile. 'Sorry, I'm really not pulling my weight in this relationship right now.'

'Claire, you're so busy you barely have time to breathe. I'm not going to give you a hard time about that; I just want to take some of the weight off your shoulders,' he said.

'Then thank you. Coffee would be lovely.'

He made two mugs of coffee and set them on the table. 'This is decaf,' he said, 'because I think you're already going to have enough trouble getting to sleep and the last thing you need is caffeine.'

'I guess.'

And he hoped that what he was about to do would distract her enough to let her fall asleep in his arms tonight and stop worrying quite so much about the wedding show.

He rescued the box he'd stowed in her fridge earlier —a box containing a very important message. He checked behind the door that he hadn't accidentally disturbed the contents of the box and mixed up the order of the lettered chocolates, then brought them out and placed the box on the table in front of her.

She gave him a tired smile. 'Would these be some of your awesome salted caramels? Or are you trying out new stuff on me as your personal focus group?'

'Open the box and see,' he invited.

She did so, and her eyes widened as she read the message. When she looked back at him, he could see the sheen of tears in her eyes. *'Sean.'*

'Hey. They say you should say it with flowers, but I know you like to be different, so I thought I'd say it in chocolate.' He'd iced the letters himself. *I love you Claire.* He paused. 'Or maybe I just need to say it.' He swallowed hard. Funny how his throat felt as if it were filled with sand. 'I've never said this to anyone before. I love you, Claire. I think I probably have for years, but the idea of letting anyone close scared me spitless. You know you asked me what scared me? *That.* Deep down guess I was worried that I'd end up losing my partner like I lost my parents, so it was easier to keep you at a distance.'

'So what changed?' she asked.

'Capri,' he said. 'Seeing the way you just got on with things and sorted out the problems when Ashleigh's dress went missing. And then dancing with you. I really couldn't take my eyes off you—it wasn't just the song. I tried to tell myself that it was just physical attraction, but it's more than that. So very much more.'

'Oh, Sean.' She blinked back the tears.

And now he just couldn't shut up. 'And in these last few weeks, getting to know you,

I've seen you for who you really are. You're funny and you're brave and you're bossy, and you think outside the box, and—you know your speed dating question thing, about what you're looking for in a partner? I can answer that, now. I'm looking for *you*, Claire. You're everything I want.' He gave her a wry smile. 'Though my timing's a bit rubbish, given that you're up to your eyes right now.'

'Your timing's perfect,' she said softly. 'You know, I had a huge crush on you when I was fourteen, but you were my best friend's older brother, which made you off limits. And you always made me feel as if I was a nuisance.'

'You probably were, when you were a teenager.'

She laughed. 'Tell it to me straight, why don't you?'

He laughed back. 'You wouldn't have it any other way, and you know it—I love you, Claire.'

'I love you, too, Sean.' She pushed her chair back, came round to his side of the table, wrapped her arms round him and kissed him. 'Over the last few weeks I've got to know you and you're not quite who I thought you were, either. You're this human dynamo but you also think on your feet. You're not regimented and rule-bound.'

'No?'

'Well, maybe just a little bit—and you do look good in a suit.' She smiled at him. 'Though how I really like you dressed is in faded jeans, and a white shirt with the sleeves rolled up. It makes you much more touchable.'

'Noted,' he said.

He could see that she was so tired, she didn't even have the energy to drink her coffee. So he carried her to bed, cherished her, and let her fall asleep in his arms. He wasn't ready to sleep yet; it was good just to lie in the dark with her in his arms, thinking. How amazing it was that she felt the same way about him. So maybe, just maybe, this was going to work out.

CHAPTER TWELVE

ON THE MORNING of the wedding show, Claire was up before six, bustling around and double-checking things on her list.

Then her mobile phone rang. Sean couldn't tell much from Claire's end of the conversation, but her face had turned white and there was a tiny pleat above her nose that told him something was definitely wrong.

When she ended the call, she blew out a breath. 'Sorry, I'm going to have to neglect you and make a ton of phone calls now.'

'What's happened?'

'That was the modelling agency.' She closed her eyes for a moment. 'It seems that the six male models that I booked through the agency are all really good friends. They went out together for a meal last night, and they've all gone down with food poisoning so they can't do the show.'

'So the agency's going to send you some-one else?'

She shook her head. 'All their models are either already booked out or away. So they're very sorry to let me down, but it's due to cir-cumstances beyond their control and they're sure I'll understand, and of course they'll re-turn my fee.'

The sing-song, patronising tone in which she replayed the conversation told Sean just how angry Claire was—and he wasn't sur-prised. She'd been very badly let down.

'I'll just have to go through my diary and beg a few favours, and hope that I can find six men willing to stand in for the models.' She raked a hand through her hair. 'And I need to look at my list and see where I can cut a few corners, because I'll have to alter their clothes to fit the stand-ins, and…' She shook her head, looking utterly miserable.

He put his arms round her and hugged her. 'You need five. I'll do it.'

She stared at him as if the words hadn't quite sunk in. '*You'll* do it?'

'Well, obviously I don't know the first thing about a catwalk,' he said, 'so someone's going to have to teach me how to do the model walk thing. But everyone's going to be looking at the clothes and not the model in any case, so I guess that probably doesn't matter too much.'

'You'll do it,' she repeated, sounding disbelieving.

'Is it that much of a stretch to see me as a model?' he asked wryly.

'No, it's not that at all. You'd be *fabulous*. It's just that—it's a pretty public thing, standing on a catwalk at a wedding show with everyone staring at you, and it's so far from what you normally do that I thought you'd find it too embarrassing or awkward or...' She tailed off. 'Oh, my God, Sean. You'd really do that for me?'

'Yes,' he said firmly.

'Thank you.' She hugged him fiercely. 'That means I only have to find five.'

'You've already got enough to do. I'll find them for you,' he said. 'I reckon we can count on Luke and Tom, and I have a few others in mind. Just tell me the rough heights and sizes you need, and I'll ring round and sort it out.'

'Your height and build would be perfect, but I can adjust things if I need to—the men's outfits are easier to adjust than the women's, so I guess I'm lucky that it was the male models and not the female ones or the children who had to bail out on me. Sean, are you really sure about this?'

'Really,' he confirmed. 'I'm on Team Claire, remember? Now go hit that shower, I'll have coffee ready by the time you're out, and I'll start ringing round.'

She hugged him. 'Have I told you how wonderful you are? Five minutes ago it felt as if the world had ended, and now...'

'Hey—you'd do the same for me,' he pointed out.

Half an hour later, Sean had it all arranged. Luke and Tom agreed immediately to stand in, plus Tom's partner. Sean called in his best friend and his sales manager from the factory, and they all agreed to meet him and Claire at the wedding show two hours before it started, so Claire could do any last-minute necessary alterations to their outfits. Then he made Claire sit down and eat breakfast, before helping her to load everything into the van she'd hired for the day.

'Sure we've got all the wedding dresses?' he asked before he closed the van doors. 'Though I guess we're going to Earl's Court rather than Capri, so we should be OK.'

'Not funny, Sean.' She narrowed her eyes at him.

He kissed her lightly. 'That was misplaced humour and I apologise. It's all going to be fine, Claire. Just breathe and check your list.'

'Sorry, I'm being unfair and overly grouchy. Ignore me.' She looked over her list. 'Everything's ticked off and loaded, so we're ready to roll.'

'At least we've got the bumps out of the way this side of the catwalk. It's all going to be fine now.' He kissed her again. 'By the way, I meant to tell you, I've got some extra giveaways for you. Will from the office is bringing them to the show.'

'Giveaways?' Her eyes went wide. 'Oh, no. I completely forgot about giveaways. I meant to order some pens. I've been so focused on the outfits that it totally slipped my mind.'

'You have business cards?'

'Yes.'

'Grab them,' he said, 'and we'll get a production line stuffing them at the show.'

'Stuffing what?' She looked at him blankly.

'My genius girlfriend talked about wedding favours. I had some samples run up, with white organza bags and gold foil on the caramel hearts. The bag is just the right size to put your business card in as well—and don't worry about the pens. Everyone will remember the chocolate.'

'Sean, that's above and beyond.'

'No, it's supporting you,' he corrected, 'and

it also works as a test run for me, so we both win. Let's get this show on the road.'

At the wedding show, people were busy setting up exhibition stands and the place was bustling. Claire was busy measuring her new male models and doing alterations; then, when the female models arrived, she filled them in on the situation and got them to teach the men how to walk. Her stand was set up with showbooks of her designs, and her part-time shop assistant Iona was there to field enquiries and take contact details of people who were interested in having a consultation about a wedding dress. Will had brought the organza bags and chocolates with him, so Sean had a production line of people stuffing bags with the chocolates and Claire's business card. He knew how much was riding on this.

And it also worried him. Claire had already had to deal with extra problems that weren't of her making today. If this didn't go to plan, all her hard work would have been for nothing.

What he wanted to do was to make sure that the people she wanted to see her collection actually saw it. She'd already mentioned the names of some of the fashion houses who were going to be there. A little networking might just give them the push they needed to make sure they saw Claire's work.

While Claire was making last-minute fixes to the dresses, Sean slipped away quietly to find the movers and shakers of her world. Claire had just about finished by the time he returned.

'Everything OK?' he asked.

'Yes.' She smiled at him. 'You're amazing and I love you. Now go strut your stuff.'

The dresses all looked breathtaking. He knew how much work had gone into them, along with Claire's heart and soul. Please let the reviewers be kind rather than snarky, he begged silently. Please let her get the kudos she deserved. Please let the fashion houses keep their word and come to see her. Please let them give her a chance.

Claire's hands were shaking visibly. Ashleigh was sitting next to her; she took Claire's hands and held them tightly. 'Breathe. It's going to be just fine.'

'They all look amazing,' Claire's grandmother added.

'You're going to wow the lot of them,' Aunt Lou said, reaching over to pat her shoulder.

Only Jacob was silent, but Claire hadn't really expected anything from her dad; she knew that fashion shows weren't his thing.

The fact that he'd actually turned up meant that he was on her side for once—didn't it?

But finally the catwalk segment of the show began. Her collection was on first. The models came down the catwalk, one group at a time: the bride, groom and bridesmaids. Autumn. Winter. Spring. Summer. Sean, looking incredibly gorgeous in morning dress and a top hat with his vintage-inspired bride beside him; her heart skipped a beat when he caught her eye and smiled at her. The contemporary civil wedding.

And then finally, the whole collection of six stood on the stage in a tableau. Claire became aware of music, lights—and was that applause?

'You did it, love,' her grandmother said and hugged her. 'Listen to everyone clapping. They think you're as fantastic as we do.'

'We did it.' Claire was shaking with a mixture of relief and adrenaline. She swallowed hard. 'I need to get back to my stand.'

'Iona can cope for another five minutes,' Aunt Lou said with a smile. 'Just enjoy this bit.'

A woman came over to join them. 'Claire Stewart?' she asked.

Claire looked up. 'Yes.'

'Pia Verdi,' the woman introduced herself, and handed over her business card.

Claire's eyes widened as she took in the name of one of the biggest wedding dress manufacturers in the country.

'I like what I've just seen up there, and I'd like to talk to you about designing a collection for us,' Pia said. 'Obviously you won't have your diary on you now, but call my PA on Monday morning and we'll set up a meeting.'

'Thank you—I'd really like that,' Claire said.

The one thing she'd been secretly hoping for—her chance in the big league. To design a collection that would be sold internationally and would have her name on it.

She just about managed to keep it together until Sean—who'd clearly changed out of his wedding outfit at top speed—came out. He picked her up and spun her round, and she laughed.

'We did it, Sean.'

'Not me. You're the one who designed those amazing outfits.'

'But you supported me when I needed it. Thank you so, so much.' She handed him the business card and grinned her head off. 'Look who wants to talk to me next week!'

'They're offering you a job?' he asked.

'Better than that—they're asking me to talk to them about designing a collection. So I'll get my name out there, but I still get to do my brides and design one-offs as well. It's the icing on the cake. Everything I wanted. I'm so happy.'

'That's brilliant news.' He hugged her. 'I'm so proud of you, Claire. You deserve this.'

'Thanks.' She beamed at him. 'Though I'd better come down off cloud nine and get back to the stand. It's not fair to leave Iona on her own.'

'I'm so glad Pia Verdi came to see you,' he said.

She frowned as his words sank in. 'Hang on. Are you telling me you know her?'

'Um, not exactly.'

Her eyes narrowed as she looked at him. 'Sean?'

He blew out a breath. 'I just networked a bit while you were sorting stuff out, that's all.'

Claire went cold. 'You *networked*?'

'I just told her that your collection was brilliant and she needed to see it.'

Bile rose in Claire's throat as she realised what had actually happened. So much for thinking that she'd got this on her own merit. That her designs had been good enough to attract the attention of one of the biggest fashion houses.

Because Sean had intervened.

Without him talking to her, Pia Verdi probably wouldn't even have bothered coming to see Claire's collection.

And, although part of Claire knew that he'd done something really nice for her, part of her was horrified. Because what this really meant was that Sean was as overprotective as her father. Whatever Sean had said, he didn't really believe in her: he didn't think that she could make it on her own, and he thought she'd always need a bit of a helping hand. To be looked after.

Stifled.

So what she'd thought was her triumph had turned out to be nothing of the kind.

'You spoke to Pia Verdi,' she repeated. 'You told her to come and see my collection.'

He waved a dismissive hand. 'Claire, it was just a little bit of networking, that's all. You would've done the same for me.'

'No.' She shook her head. 'No, I wouldn't have thought that I needed to interfere. Because I *know* you can do things on your own. I *know* that you'll succeed without having someone to push you and support you. And you...' She blew out a breath. 'You just have to be in control. All the time. That's not what I want.'

'Claire, I—'

'No,' she cut in. 'No. I think you've just clarified something for me. Something important. I can't do this, Sean. I can't be with someone who doesn't consult me and who always plays things by the book—*his* book.' She shook her head. 'I'm sorry. I know you meant well, but…this isn't what I want.' She took a deep breath. There was no going back now. 'It's over.'

'Claire—'

She took a backward step, avoiding his outstretched hand. 'No. Goodbye, Sean.'

She walked away with her head held high. And all the time she was thinking, just how could today have turned from so spectacularly wonderful to so spectacularly terrible? How could it all have gone so wrong?

Even though her heart was breaking, she smiled and smiled at everyone who came to her exhibition stand. She talked about dresses and took notes. She refused help from everyone to pack things away at the end of the show and did it all herself; by then, her anger had burned out to leave nothing but sadness. Sean had taken her at her word and left, which was probably for the best; but her stupid heart still wished that he were there with her.

Well, too late. It was over—and they were too different for it to have worked out long term. So this summer had just been a fling. One day she'd be able to look back on it and remember the good times, but all she could think of now was the bitterness of her disappointment and how she wished he'd been the man she thought he was.

Stupid, stupid, *stupid*.

Sean hated himself for the way the light had gone from Claire's eyes. Because he'd been the one to cause it. He'd burst her bubble big-time—ruined the exuberance she'd felt at her well-deserved success. He'd meant well—he'd talked to Pia Verdi and the others with the best possible intentions—but now he could see that he'd done completely the wrong thing. He'd taken it all away from Claire, and he'd made her feel as if the bottom had dropped out of her world.

It felt as if the bottom had fallen out of his world, too. He'd lost something so precious. He knew it was all his own fault; and he really wasn't sure he was ever going to be able to fix this.

He definitely couldn't fix it today; he knew

he needed to give her time to cool down. But tomorrow he'd call her. Apologise. Really lay his heart on the line—and hope that she'd forgive him and give him a second chance.

CHAPTER THIRTEEN

IT SHOULD HAVE been a night of celebration.

Not wanting to jinx things before the wedding show, Claire hadn't booked a table at a restaurant in advance; though she'd planned to take her family, Sean, Ashleigh and Luke out to dinner that evening, to thank them for all the support they'd given her in the run-up to the show.

But now the food would just taste like ashes; and she didn't want her misery to infect anyone else. So she smiled and smiled and lied her face off to her family and her best friend, pretending that her heart wasn't breaking at all. 'I'm fine. Anyway, I need to get the van back to the hire company, and start sorting out all these enquiries…'

Finally she persuaded them all to stop worrying about her, and left in the van on her own. But, by the time she'd dropped all the outfits back at her shop, delivered the van back to the hirer and caught the tube back to her flat, she felt drained and empty. Dinner was a glass of milk—which was just about all she could face—and she lay alone in her bed, dry-eyed and too miserable to sleep and wishing that things were different.

Had she been unfair to Sean?

Or were her fears—that he'd be overprotective and stifling in the future, and they'd be utterly miserable together—justified?

Claire still hadn't worked it out by the time she got up at six, the next morning. It was ridiculously early for a Sunday, but there was no point in just lying there and brooding. Though she felt like death warmed up after yet another night of not sleeping properly, and it took three cups of coffee with extra sugar before she could function enough to take a shower and wash her hair.

Work seemed to be about the best answer. If she concentrated on sketching a new design, she wouldn't have room in the front of her head to think about what had happened with Sean. And maybe the back of her head would come up with some answers.

She hoped.

She was sketching in her living room when her doorbell rang.

Odd. She wasn't expecting anyone to call.

And she hadn't replied to any of the messages on her phone yet, so as far as everyone else was concerned she was probably still asleep, exhausted after the wedding show.

And who would ring her doorbell before half past eight on a Sunday morning, anyway?

She walked downstairs and blinked in surprise when she opened the door.

Sean was standing there—dressed in jeans and a white shirt rather than his normal formal attire—and he was carrying literally an armful of flowers. She could barely see him behind all the blooms and the foliage of delphiniums, stocks, gerberas and roses.

She blinked at him. 'Sean?'

'Can I come in?' he asked.

'I…' Help. What did she say now?

'I'll say what I've got to say on your doorstep, if I have to,' he said. 'But I'd rather talk to you in private.'

She wasn't too sure that she wanted an audience, either. 'Come up,' she said, and stood aside so he could go past and she could close the door behind them.

'Firstly,' he said, 'I wanted to say sorry. And these are just…' He stopped, glanced down at the flowers and then at her. 'I've gone over the top, haven't I?'

'They're gorgeous—though I'm not sure if

I have enough vases, glasses and mugs to fit them all in,' she said.

'I just wanted to say sorry. And I kind of thought I needed to make a big gesture, because the words aren't quite enough. And I know you love flowers. And...' His voice trailed off.

'You're carrying an entire English cottage garden there.' She was still hurt that he didn't truly believe in her, but she could see how hard he was trying to start making things right. And as he stood there in the middle of all the flowers, looking completely like a fish out of water...how could she stay angry with him?

'Let's get these gorgeous flowers in water before they start wilting.' She went into the kitchen and found every receptacle she had, and started filling them with water. 'They're lovely. Thank you. Where did you get them?' she asked. 'Covent Garden flower market isn't open on Sundays.'

'Columbia Road market,' he said. 'I looked up where I could get really good fresh flowers first thing on a Sunday morning.'

She thought about it. 'So you carried all these on the tube?'

'Uh-huh.' He gave her a rueful smile. 'I had to get someone to help me at the ticket barrier.'

He'd gone to a real effort for her. And he'd done something that would've made people stare at him—something she knew would've made him feel uncomfortable.

So this apology was sincerely meant. But she still needed to hear the words.

When they'd finished putting the flowers in water—including using the bowl of her kitchen sink—she said, 'Do you want a coffee?'

'No, thanks. I just need to talk to you,' he said. He took a deep breath. 'Claire, I honestly didn't mean to hurt you. I just wanted to help. But I realise now that I handled it totally the wrong way. I interfered instead of supporting you properly and asking you what you needed me to do. I made you feel as if you were hopeless and couldn't do anything on your own but, Claire, I *do* believe in you. I knew your designs would make any of the fashion houses sit up and take notice. But the wedding show was so busy, I didn't want to take the risk that they wouldn't get time to see your collection and you wouldn't get your chance. That's the only reason I went to talk to Pia Verdi.'

His expression was serious and completely sincere. She knew he meant what he said.

And she also knew that she owed him an apology, too. They were *both* in the wrong.

'I overreacted a bit as well,' she said. 'I'd been working flat out for weeks and, after the way everything had gone wrong from the first…well, I think it just caught me at the wrong time. Now I've had time to think about it, I know your heart was in the right place. You meant well. But yesterday I felt that you were being overprotective and stifling, the way Dad is, because you don't think I can do it on my own. You think that I need looking after all the time.'

'Claire, I'm not your father. I know you can do it on your own,' he said softly. 'And, for the record, I don't think you need looking after. Actually, I think it would drive you bananas.'

'It would.' She took a deep breath. 'I want an equal partnership with someone who'll back me and who'll let me back them.'

'That's what I want, too,' Sean said.

Hope bloomed in her heart. 'Before yesterday—before things went wrong—that's what I thought we had,' she said.

'We did,' he said. 'We *do*.'

She bit her lip. 'I've hurt you as much as you hurt me. I was angry and unfair and ungrateful, I pushed you away, and I'm sorry. And, if I try to think first instead of reacting first in future, do you think we could start again?'

'So Ms Follow-Your-Heart turns into a rulebook devotee?' Sean said. 'No deal. Because I want a partner who thinks outside the box and stops me being regimented.'

'You're not regimented—well, not *all* the time,' she amended.

'Thank you. I think.' He looked at her. 'I can't promise perfection and I can't promise we won't ever fight again, Claire.'

'It wouldn't be normal if we didn't ever fight again,' she pointed out.

'True. I guess we just need to learn to compromise. Do things the middle way instead of both thinking that our way's the only way.' He opened his arms. 'So. You and me. How about it?'

She stepped into his arms. 'Yes.'

'Good.' He kissed her lingeringly. 'And we'll talk more in future. I promise I won't think I know best.'

'And I promise I won't go super-stubborn.'

He laughed. 'Maybe we ought to qualify that and say we'll *try*.'

'Good plan.'

He arched an eyebrow. 'Are you going to admit that planning's good, outside business?'

She laughed. 'That would be a no. Most of the time. Are you going to admit that being spontaneous means you have more fun?'

He grinned. 'Not if I'm hungry and I've just been drenched in a downpour.'

'Compromise,' she said. 'That works for me.'

'Me, too.' He kissed her again. 'And we'll make this work. Together.'

EPILOGUE

Two months later

CLAIRE WAS WORKING on the preliminary sketches for her first collection for Pia Verdi when her phone beeped.

She glanced at the screen. Sean. Probably telling her that he was going to be late home tonight, she thought with a smile. Although they hadn't officially moved in with each other, they'd fallen into a routine of spending weeknights at her place and weekends at his.

V and A. Thirty minutes. Be there.

Was he kidding?

Three tube changes! Takes thirty minutes PLUS walk to station, she typed back.

And of course he'd know she knew this. The Victoria and Albert Museum was her favourite place in London. She'd taken him there several times and always lingered in front of her favourite dress, a red grosgrain and chiffon dress by Chanel. She never, ever tired of seeing that dress.

Forty minutes, then.

Half a minute later, there was another text.

Make it fifty and change into your blue dress. The one with the daisies.

Why?

Tell you when you get here.

She grinned. Sean was clearly in playful mode, so this could be fun. But why did he want to meet her at the museum? And why that dress in particular?

She still didn't have a clue when she actually got to Kensington. She texted him from the museum entrance: Where are you?

Right next to your favourite exhibit.

Easy enough, she thought, and went to find him.

He was standing next to the display case,

dressed up to the nines: a beautifully cut dark suit and a white shirt, but for once he wasn't wearing a tie. That little detail was enough to soften the whole package. Just how she liked it.

'OK. I'm here.' She gestured to her outfit. 'Blue dress. Daisies. As requested, Mr Farrell.'

'You look beautiful,' he said.

'Thank you. But I'm still trying to work out why you wanted to meet me here.'

'Because I'm just about to add to your workload.'

She frowned. 'I don't understand.'

He dropped to one knee. 'Claire Stewart, I love you with all my heart. Will you marry me?'

'I…' She stared at him. 'Sean. I can't quite take this in. You're really asking me to marry you?'

'I'm down on one knee and I used the proper form,' he pointed out.

This was the last thing she'd expected on a Thursday afternoon in her favourite museum. 'Sean.'

'I've been thinking about it for the last month. Where else could you ask a wedding dress designer to marry you, except in her favourite place in London? And next to her favourite exhibit, too?'

Now she knew why he'd asked her to wear his favourite dress: to make this just as special for him. And why he'd said he was adding to her workload—because now she'd have a very special wedding dress to design. Her own.

She smiled. 'Sean Farrell, I love you with all my heart, too. And I'd be thrilled to marry you.'

He stood up, swung her round, and kissed her thoroughly. Then he took something from his pocket. 'We need to formalise this.'

She blinked. 'You bought me a ring?'

'Without consulting you? No chance. This is temporary. Go with the flow. *Carpe diem*,' he said, and slid something onto the ring finger of her left hand.

When she looked at it, she burst out laughing. He'd made her a ring out of unused toffee wrappers.

'We'll choose the proper one together,' he said. 'Just as we'll make all our important decisions together.'

'An equal partnership,' she said, and kissed him. 'Perfect.'

* * * * *

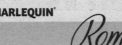

LARGER-PRINT BOOKS!

GET 2 FREE LARGER-PRINT NOVELS PLUS
2 FREE GIFTS!

◆ HARLEQUIN®

Romance

From the Heart, For the Heart

YES! Please send me 2 FREE LARGER-PRINT Harlequin® Romance novels and my 2 FREE gifts (gifts are worth about $10). After receiving them, if I don't wish to receive any more books, I can return the shipping statement marked "cancel." If I don't cancel, I will receive 4 brand-new novels every month and be billed just $4.84 per book in the U.S. or $5.24 per book in Canada. That's a savings of at least 19% off the cover price! It's quite a bargain! Shipping and handling is just 50¢ per book in the U.S. and 75¢ per book in Canada.* I understand that accepting the 2 free books and gifts places me under no obligation to buy anything. I can always return a shipment and cancel at any time. Even if I never buy another book, the two free books and gifts are mine to keep forever.

119/319 HDN F43Y

Name	(PLEASE PRINT)

Address	Apt. #

City	State/Prov.	Zip/Postal Code

Signature (if under 18, a parent or guardian must sign)

Mail to the **Harlequin® Reader Service:**
IN U.S.A.: P.O. Box 1867, Buffalo, NY 14240-1867
IN CANADA: P.O. Box 609, Fort Erie, Ontario L2A 5X3
Want to try two free books from another line?
Call 1-800-873-8635 or visit www.ReaderService.com.

HRLP13R

"I'm not divorcing you," Jessica said. "We're divorcing each other. Isn't that what you want?"

Kade found where her sling was discarded on the floor and looped it gently over her head.

"It seems to be what you want, all of a sudden," he said. "There's something you aren't telling me, isn't there?"

She felt suddenly weak, as if she could blurt out her deepest secret to him. How would it feel to tell him? *Kade, there is going to be a baby after all.*

No, that was not the type of thing to blurt out. What would be her motivation? Did she think it would change things between them? She didn't want them to change because of a baby. She wanted them to change because he loved her.

What? She didn't want things to change between them at all. She was taking steps to close this door, not reopen it! She was happy.

"Happy, happy, happy," she muttered out loud.

"Huh?"

"Oh. Just thinking out loud."

He looked baffled, as well he should!

"Go to bed," he told her. "We'll talk later. Now is obviously not the time."

He had that right! Where were these thoughts coming from? She needed to get her defenses back up.

With what seemed to be exquisite tenderness, he slipped her cast back inside the sling, adjusted the knot on the back of her neck.

His touch made her feel hungry for him and miss him more than it seemed possible. He put his hand on her left elbow and helped her up, and then across the bathroom and into the bedroom.

He let go of her only long enough to turn back the bedclothes and help her slide into the bed.

He tucked the covers up around her and stood looking down at her.

"Okay," she said, "I'm fine. You can leave."

He started to go, but then he turned back and stood in the bedroom door, one big shoulder braced against the frame.

He looked at her long and hard, until the ache came back so strong she had to clamp her teeth together to keep herself from flicking open the covers, an invitation.

Don't miss
THE PREGNANCY SECRET by Cara Colter,
available May 2015 wherever
Harlequin® Romance books and ebooks are sold.

www.Harlequin.com